Jane George

FOR THE MUSKRAT

AUTHOR'S NOTE

This is a work of fiction and all names and places are either entirely fictitious or are used fictitiously. Although many of the place details are accurate to New York City in 1980, this story is not intended to be a faithful chronicle of the music club scene at that time. What follows is a tale of outsiders, phonies who are nevertheless real phonies, drawn to New York, like generations of searchers before them, in a quest for authenticity and validation.

Thanks go to Diane Reverand, Esri Allbritten, and Gwendolyn Heasley for suggestions and revisions that greatly improved this story.

CHAPTER ONE

San Francisco
June, 1980

Fate loves a doorbell. Me, not so much, but it is my party so I run to answer the door. I sock-slide down the hallway, shriek, and bang into the wall. Bright purple hair dye splatters the yellowed wallpaper leaving fluorescent trails across my vision. The Cure's *Fire in Cairo* plays. Loud. Dye drips down the wall and my face.

"Come on, don't trash the place because you're leaving," says Alicia, my fellow squatter. We were paying rent to her boyfriend until he got involved in some kind of property dispute. The free lodging allowed me to save cash for New York.

I laugh, and to my ears it sounds like bells.

I don't owe her a reply. I don't owe her anything, yet I say, "Alicia, the invite said, *'J.J.'s Dye-your-hair-and–drop-acid Going Away Party.'* So if you're not going to do either, go away." I don't know my guests much or at all. Who better to see me off than people who don't care?

"Grow up," she says.

I'm a legal adult. Just. However, Alicia never lets me forget my history as an 'unofficially emancipated minor,' as my mom put it. Mom ran out of gas on the parenting thing when I was fifteen.

Since then it's been sink or swim. I've done both.

Alicia collects the mail bag she uses as a purse and heads toward the door. Turning around, she adds, "How come none of your *usual* friends are here?"

"Why would I invite the people I'm running away from?" I laugh again, more like icicle wind chimes this time. "New York should be far enough away, don'tcha think?"

"New York, New York, *New York*," she says. My grubby copy of *The Basketball Diaries* flies across the entryway and smacks me in the chest. "You're way too pretentious to be a punk rocker, you know. "

In retaliation, I launch her terry cloth headband. It hits her boob.

Alicia smiles a just-one-more-day-and-she's-gone smile. "Goodbye, J.J. Try not to wake me when the taxi picks you up in the morning."

As Alicia edges out into the entry, the two bell-ringers make their way to the door. I squint; the lights are spinning. I recognize Art Munny. I gave him my number two weeks ago because he plays guitar in a band.

He looks like a junkie version of the Clash's guitarist. I'll never touch the stuff. But heroin-loving rock stars live as the fragile gods and goddesses of my universe, as cool as white spiders, creatures unaffected by mere realities of gravity and sunlight. However, Art is a straight-up, serious musician with a day job in insurance, and allergies that cause dark circles under his eyes.

Art holds out his arms to me. He takes in my appearance and drops them again.

"Ah, J.J.," he says. "This is my roommate Michael. Michael this is J.J."

I look through Michael. "You brought a straight geek to my party?" I shake my head. Bad idea. More purple drips. "Beer, wine and chips are in the kitchen." I wave them through, shut the door, and turn all the deadbolts.

"Are we your prisoners?" asks Michael. In this light, he looks like Elvis Costello. My opinion thaws.

"Naw, some people here have taken three hits of Windowpane and they keep trying to go outside," I say and catch Michael giving Art a *what the hell have you gotten me into?* look.

Later, I trap Michael on the sofa by sitting on the coffee table and throwing my army-booted feet onto the overstuffed arm. Art scowls trendily in a doorway, chatting up a girl in a new-wave mini-skirt.

"Is she going home with him?" I ask Michael and stuff a tortilla chip in my mouth.

Uneasiness flits across his face and is gone. "Maybe in a parallel universe."

"Parallel universe?" Someone drops a dish in the kitchen. I ignore it even though the noise crashes through my bones.

"Yeah," he risks a nervous smile. "Just like this one, by way of the road not taken."

I crunch another chip. "How many universes are there, then?"

With a glance at Art, Michael laughs. "As many as necessary."

"My head is burning," I say. "This shit hurts."

He blinks once. "Is it time to wash it off?"

I look at the clock. "About three hours ago. Help me?"

In the bathroom, I lean over the cracked, claw-foot tub while Michael, all elbows, rinses my hair with the handheld sprayer. Tentatively, he pats my head with a towel and then wraps it up turban style. He stands back to review his work like a nuclear physicist who has just roped a calf. Satisfied, he pushes his Buddy Holly glasses back up his nose. His fingers are purple. Strands of hair fall messily over his forehead. Cute.

My scalp still hurts. Do guys who like Elvis Costello and parallel universes dig bald chicks?

"Can I, er, call you, sometime, maybe? From New York?" I ask him.

Michael adjusts his glasses again. "Uh, yeah sure, I guess."

* * *

3

New York City
June, 1980

On my first night in New York, I get ready for a nocturnal jaunt. My clothes are draped over the metal bed frame in my dormitory style room in the YMCA hostel on Thirty-Fourth Street. I can't decide if the bed and room shout *army barracks* or *Depression-era hospital.* Either way, my costume is wrong. But still I play dress-up. The *Voice* is spread on the mattress, open to the live acts listings. Without my club-going coterie, I have no clue which venues are in. CBGB and Mudd Club are over, or so I hear. I can't risk jinxing my new city by looking like I'm trying to jump a passé train. I choose a classic, The Peppermint Lounge.

Luckily, I escaped the punishment of baldness for my beauty supply store binge at my going away party. My hair screams purple, not solid purple, but a serendipitous layering of white blond roots, a rich plum in the middle, and tips of jet black. I squeeze a generous amount of cheap hair gel into my palm, and torture the short strands as best I can. Even cut short, it refuses to spike in proper punk fashion. And I'm fresh out of egg whites.

I draw up my lip in an imitation of a Sid Vicious sneer. The resultant snort catches in my throat. I cough. New York will have to take me as I am. With my huge eyes, aristocratic nose, and stubborn hair, I always end up looking like a magical bird out *of A Midsummer Night's Dream,* no matter what color my hair is.

New town, old clothes. The vintage lace flapper's dress is my uniform. I retrieve it from the bed and wriggle into it. Green army boots follow. The finishing touch is a black and silver fringed scarf I wind around my head, pulling spikes of hair through it like thorns.

At nine p.m., I leave to see the act at the Peppermint Lounge, the historic home of Chubby Checker and the Twist. I walk into a world of shiny black surfaces and red neon, but the place is empty of the chic underground patrons I imagine. Is the headlining band awful? Will I live this down?

I clutch my small duffle bag to my chest and sit on the base of a column near the corner. Maybe no one will notice me. The doorman, who didn't bother to check my ID, sticks his finger in the bouncer's ribs. They both look my way and grin. I'm as pathetic and obvious as Oliver Twist.

The bartender picks up on the joke as he dries a glass. With his elbow, he gestures to a large, debonair black man in a suit with wide lapels.

The man swivels on his stool. "Hi there, sweet thing. Care for a tour around Manhattan?"

I spin away to face the wall, and the men erupt into laughter behind my back.

The show finally starts. The opening band truly is dreadful. Impatient, I stand and work my way around the club by slinking along the wall.

It isn't as if New York is a foreign country. The problem must be with me. I still haven't figured out how to order a cup of coffee here. Coffee light, dark, sweet, it makes no sense. This morning I wanted to scream at the lady behind the counter to just make it black and point me to the cream and sugar, I'd do it myself. But here in New York they do that for you, if you know the magic words.

A man accidentally on purpose bumps into me.

"You do not look like other American girls," he says with a light French accent.

I narrow my eyes, heavy with eyeliner and mascara I've slept in and re-applied for three days straight. "Thanks."

The guy looks a little like a continental Paul McCartney.

He says, "I am here in New York from Paris. I sell linoleum flooring."

"Nice."

He buys me a drink. He buys me another drink.

I stay near the dark wall and loathe myself. *J.J. the polite punk rocker.* I should spit on the floor. But I can't. He presses me to the wall and kisses me. The urge to bite him, savage not sexual, flames up. I kiss him back instead.

He pulls away from my mouth. "You are ze only girl I have met here who uses her tongue."

Bra-vo. My soul disengages from my body, passing a bitter cloud of vodka-stale breath on its way out.

"Are you feeling okay?" he asks.

"*Comme çi, comme ça.*" I try the Sid Vicious sneer again.

"Oh no, no," he responds with a pained look. "I am here to improve my English. We speak only English."

We go back to the Y, where I know the doorman won't let him come upstairs with me.

"I need to go up and get something. I'll be right back down," I lie. I hurry into the elevator. A new town, a new me. Back in San Francisco, I would have gone home with that asshole and it would have been horrible. I don't worry about missing anything, each of my sexual experiences has been worse than the last, and nothing close to an orgasm has ever surfaced.

In my room, feeling guilty, I change into a sleep tee and imagine the forlorn French dog on the pavement below. He won't wait long. He was only hoping to use me to polish his English and his penis. My thoughts turn to what I should do tomorrow in this tall and callous city. I should go for a run. My body aches to sprint, to stretch its legs and fly. Is there a safe time to jog in Central Park? New Yorkers are largely immune to purple hair, but an *exercising* punk girl will be certain to attract attention.

I need a job, two, in order to survive here. I ran away from them, the people Alicia had called my "usual" friends. Hah, not even Voodoo and his black yarn trouble dolls can find me in a city this big.

I roll over and fall asleep, my animal instincts on alert in a strange place.

A moaning in the hallway wakes me. Something bumps the door near to the ground. The groans and sobs lodge there, as if a forsaken shade, or demon, who has tarried too long above ground, cannot return to Hades because the gates are shut.

Should I open the door? I think about knives, and crazy people. I long to sleep. Incessant cries and moans, bumps and jerks, continue against the door. Where is the night watchman? How can a demon end up on the hallway of the Young Men's Christian Association?

Of all the people lodging at the Y, I am singled out. There is a reason this nut has chosen my door. I am defective. I teased and abandoned a French linoleum salesman.

Crying now, I bang my head on the wall in synchronization with the thumps against the door.

New York
August, 1980

The young man struggles to get his bicycle through the double doors in the building entry to my hard-won, ground floor flat on Fifth Street between Avenues A and B, in the Lower East Side area known as Alphabet City. Timid, I stand and watch him. His face, flushed red with embarrassment, creates a stark contrast with his lank, white-blonde hair, which falls forward and covers every feature except for his mouth.

I let him wrestle with his bicycle while I survey his lips, which are wide and full yet don't cross over into the obscenity of excess. I've only encountered such curves and dips in museums, on mouths carved of marble.

"Is it you who has the ad? For the roommate?" he asks.

He sets his bicycle against the stairwell and flips his hair out of his face. His messenger's bag slips around and bangs him in the chest. He reddens again and turns the tables by staring acutely back at me. His face arrests all preconceptions, captures my heart and aesthetic sensibilities on the spot. My arms quiver, and I feel stupid. He is beautiful. I ache for him, like looking at a postcard of Paris and knowing it's likely I'll never go. I don't even know his name.

I nod in response, and we enter the apartment I can't afford. Even with two jobs, I need a roommate.

Once the residence of a turn-of-the-century physician, the dwelling charms with decayed elegance. The doctor's rat-infested offices in the basement are now home to a pair of party hearty boys from Alabama, who have their own construction company. With their jumpsuits and helmets, it's like having Devo-with-a-drawl living down there.

In my apartment, floor to ceiling shuttered windows face the street in the living room and a non-working fireplace graces one wall. "This room is mine," I tell the applicant.

"Is the middle room taken?"

"Consider it yours." I lean against the wall, eyes focused on the floor.

He cranes his neck sideways to get a better look at me. "Hold your chin up," he commands in a gentle tone. "Just like that. You're not going to believe this." He runs to his messenger's bag, pulls out a dog-eared sketchbook, and then flops cross-legged on the floor. "Look at these, you are the first girl I've met who looks just like my drawings." With excitement, on the hardwood floor he places sheets of paper filled with masterful, spidery sketches.

Haughty, idealized fashion faces frown at me from every page, their poses languid and life-like. Spare lines express the grace of neck and collarbone. The artist did not shy away from the difficulty of hands and fingers. Each face is John Singer Sargent's *Madame X*. Each face is me.

Am I flattered? I seethe with jealousy. My tortured attempts at art fill one corner of the room. His drawings are superb, so lovely I could tear them up, and I can tell they come straight from his head, the human figure rendered brilliantly from memory.

I sigh. "If you're going to live here, I should know your name."

He points to the repeating signatures on the scattered pieces of paper. *X-It.*

"I'm J.J. Buckingham." I cross the room with echoing footsteps. "X-It, would you care to see the view?"

X-It gathers up his lifeblood, returns it to the sketchbook, and then stands next to me. I appraise him as compact, muscular, and graceful. He is five foot eight, just right for my five foot two inches.

I let in the unforgiving August sunlight. Only two of the buildings on the opposite side of the street are not burned and gutted. They house shooting galleries. Entranced, I have already watched the addicts trail to the buildings like ants to bait.

"The shooting gallery on the right appears to cater solely to Puerto Rican clientele," I explain. "The other is indiscriminate."

X-It blinks his pale eyes in the glare. I close the shutters.

I turn and say, "So far not one of the junkies looks anything like a rock star, but maybe…someday."

CHAPTER TWO

New York
October, 1980

Glorious, autumn-gilded Manhattan unfolds before me as I gaze north up Madison Avenue. My feet, firm on the pavement on either side of my rusty bicycle steed, steady me as I regain my breath.

"Come on," shouts X-It, impatient. He maneuvers around vehicles with ease and confidence.

I mount and edge out into traffic at the same moment a city bus belches diesel and lurches forward. The driver lays on the horn and glares at me. I send a shaky smile toward X-It and pedal forward.

"You go in front," he orders. "I better keep an eye on you before you get killed. And watch out for taxis and car doors."

Riding bikes up to Central Park is X-It's idea. Never overconfident and happiest on my own two feet, I agreed to the scheme to please him.

X-it points with glee to the street corner. "I saw Andy Warhol right there, last Wednesday," he says as if he'll win a prize. If junkies are my mysterious muse, Andy Warhol is X-It's.

My bicycle wheels touch the path into the park. I exhale a sigh of relief. Maybe X-It won't be too disappointed if I walk my bike home.

He swoops in front of me and bounces along the terrain beside the paved lane, standing on his pedals. His corded arms control his destiny. I stare at the muscling beneath his clothes. Life as a bicycle messenger denies him any fat.

I struggle to keep up with him. The path undulates, rises and falls. I'm aware of not meeting his standards. Why do I care? X-It is my best friend. We do our laundry together. He's fascinating, shiny, over-talented, sinuous. I love him.

As far as any kind of romantic relationship goes, I constantly search for clues as to what my next move should be, but he doesn't give any.

I catch up to him and we top a rise together. He speeds ahead on the descent. His laughter trails behind him like amused exhaust. I smile, and a middle-aged man on a park bench calls out, "Ah. Young love."

Does the man see something I don't? I hope so, yet his words ring ironic and false, as powerless as my legs, which exert so much wasted pressure on a bicycle with no gears.

The sun plays hide-and-seek behind cumulus cotton. Sweaty, X-It and I flop on the grassy meadow. He's careful not to invade my space. I turn on my side and survey him lying some six feet away as he stares into the homey comfort of the calico canopy of leaves.

His abdomen stretches taut as he lies relaxed. His quadriceps bulge slightly, testing corduroy strength. His profile, uneventful in beginning and middle, is punctuated at the end with the exclamation mark of his incredible lips. God, he's beautiful. Shivers creep into places I've been denying. Maybe with him I could actually enjoy sex.

"You know what I want to do?" he asks.

I startle. "What?"

"I want to push around one of those Popsicle carts with bells. You and I could do this together. Depending on the season, we'd have a specific flavor pop of the day, homemade from fresh juice. And you know what?"

"No, what?"

"We'd dye our hair to match. Everyone in the park would know who we were. They wouldn't even have to ask us what flavor we had, on what day, they'd just look at our hair."

I giggle, roll on my belly, and pull apart a dandelion gone to seed.

"I'm serious." He pouts.

"It would be a lot of work. You might get bored with the concept."

He's on one of his creative rants. It's hard to stop him when he gets like this.

"Then we should form our own art co-op, nothing would be signed by individuals, just stamped with the co-op logo. Maybe call it something deep and bottomless, like Ocean, or obscure, like Chance Studio."

I sit up. "Yeah!" I always have trouble signing my work, anyway. Too much commitment. Oh, I do love him.

"Only," he says still staring up at the clouds. "You'll have to improve your draftsmanship. Quite a bit."

His words slap my face. I stand then stumble over to my bicycle.

I mumble to the meadow, "I'm working both jobs tomorrow, I think I'll head home. I'm going to walk."

He remains prone on the grass. "Good plan. You're not allowed to die until Ocean is famous." He says it lightly, but at least he cares.

I walk my corroded nag through the Upper West Side, a neighborhood I like but can never be a part of. Geraniums on Brownstone steps beneath lace-curtained windows gag me with their sentimental conformity. I long to be able to yearn for such a life, but it would ruin my cool. Suddenly ill at ease in my torn striped leggings and black lace mini dress, I increase my speed and stride south.

In Hell's Kitchen, a large homeless woman sits leaning against a black-red brick wall.

"Spare change, Missy?" she asks.

I'm not used to being accosted by bums, being only a rung or two higher on the ladder of fringe elements myself. I pull up short.

"I don't have any money." A thought spreads over me. "Hey, do you want my bike?"

A stereotypical gap-toothed smile fills the woman's face. I stretch out my arms, try to squeeze my nostrils shut, and push the handlebars toward the rising vagrant.

The woman pedals away, and I'm rewarded by her happy cackles. Free, I practically skip home on my own two feet.

* * *

The next morning, like all weekday mornings, I ride the Fourteenth Street line over into Williamsburg to paint faces on mannequins. After exiting at Bedford, I buy one large Granny Smith apple for lunch from the Polish grocer. I then take an industrial elevator to the fifth floor of a cavernous warehouse, sidle past rows of stilted, affected gestures from the dangling fiberglass arms and legs, and sit on my stool next to the brick wall, which lets in trickles of water when it rains.

My job is to give features to the blank, bald heads. Only my skill can grace them with arching eyebrows, pouty lips, and eyes that focus.

I embrace a torso with my left arm and balance it on my lap, carefully avoiding its breasts. The work is tedious. Mistakes are frowned upon. No creativity is allowed in choice of eye, lip, or make-up colors. Every mannequin comes down from above with an index card that dictates its artistic particulars.

All of the mannequins are sculpted from live fashion models by the sensitive hands of an elderly, Eastern European gentleman who long ago gave up his dreams. I labor with the other five-dollars-an-hour elves as we sit awkwardly on our stools and wrestle with the armless top halves of fashion models who look, without their wigs, as though they are undergoing chemotherapy.

The lunch whistle blows. I bring out my apple and my pet project, a broken-off mannequin head I retrieved from the trash bin. The head's name is Karisma, and its real-life fleshy counterpart, barely a year older than me, is on the covers of three fashion magazines this month. I haven't painted features on the bodiless head. Instead, I banish her baldness with an intricate, elaborate Art Deco headdress from the era and time I wish I could've come to New York.

"You do that every day," says one of the elves, pointing to Karisma's head. "Don't you want to come downstairs and stretch your legs with us?"

"No, thanks." If X-It could time travel, would he choose to be part of Andy Warhol's Factory in the Sixties? Will future generations pine to be part of the punk and new wave scenes at CBGB's and the Mudd Club? My co-worker gives up and goes away.

The plastics, resins, and spray paint that perfume the fifth floor are stronger than airplane glue. After work, I descend into the subway high as a huffer. I take a breath and instead fill my lungs with the oily must and piss of the subway.

At the Eighth Avenue station, on the Manhattan side of the river, the train doors slide open. On the white-tiled wall is a chalkboard with an authorized, blocky-figured chalk drawing. Legal graffiti. There is a different one each week. A real artist, who works in the cloakroom at the new Dance-o-Matic club, draws them.

Annoyed and holding my breath, I trudge up the stairs to the street and grab a deep lungful of street exhaust in an attempt to dispel the mannequin and underground fumes. By the time I reach my second job, I feel fairly normal.

At the trendy Chelsea bakery where I work evenings, I tie my apron around my waist. Through the window, I see X-It pull up on his bicycle. I shove an over-thick, over-rich brownie into the hand of a young urban professional who looks like he's already consumed too much caffeine, and I run outside.

"Hey," X-It says, his lips threatening to render me speechless. "Meet me at the midtown multiplex. Jacques Tati festival tonight."

Without waiting for my reply, he takes off downtown at incredible speed. My heart flies after him.

X-It's choice of theater makes me smile. I'll be able to walk past the department stores on Fifth Avenue. I don't look at the clothes. I look for my mannequins. I can tell which ones are the ones I paint. They smile back at me. With stylish clothes, hair and shoes, the dummies are different creatures than the frigid sex dolls who leave the warehouse bubble-wrapped and boxed.

When I go to meet X-It after work, he stands on the corner outside the theater. He bounces on his toes, his hands in his pockets. His slash of white-blond hair swings across his face. He looks up and sees me, his eyes bright. My heart bucks like I had too much coffee. But I didn't have any.

He blurts out, "Guess what I'm going to do, all next week? If I like it, I'll do it all month."

I wait in silence for him to elaborate.

"I'm going to dress only in red and blue for work. Get it? Only red and blue."

I stare at the sidewalk. "O-kay."

He gives me his look that says I continually need to be brought up to speed. "When I wear red and blue, I'll make a blur of primary colors as I ride on my bike through the yellow taxicabs." He nods with excitement.

I give him a Mona Lisa smile and look at my shoes, but I admire him. A lot. His job as a Manhattan bicycle messenger has the modern danger level equivalent of the Pony Express. That he can turn such a vocation into active performance art is astonishing. My mannequins suddenly look like the fakes they are.

We're early for the show. The lobby contains very few patrons and a huge expanse of lurid purple and blue carpeting. He pays, takes my hand, and leads me to the center of the lobby. All I think about is the touch of his fingers on mine.

"Stand here. Close your eyes, and hold out your hands," he says.

I do as he asks. I am being showered with paper. No, not paper, I realize as I open my eyes.

Dazzling golden leaves rain out of his messenger's bag. Feather-light, fresh and spicy, the leaves keep coming down. Upon my head. Into my palms. Onto the purple-blue carpet, where they stick in perfect chromic contrast.

X-It's eyes glitter. "Happy Fall, J.J.!"

He's magical. He is everything I ever wanted to be. I move to throw my arms about him, but he holds out his bag and shakes it, making sure all the leaves are out.

I take a step back.

We walk home after the film. X-It veers away from me, drawn to a newsstand by the image of Karisma smiling from several magazine covers at once.

"She's so perfect," he says.

I grit my teeth, yet straighten my spine in an effort to measure up.

"And here's Brooke Shields in her Calvins. Incredible. Who do you think is more beautiful?"

I think Brooke looks like a gilded giraffe-child, but that doesn't prevent me from envying every inch of Miss Shields. I want to scream at X-It, "Look at me! I'm beautiful! And I'm just your size!"

But I say, "I don't know. We don't have a mannequin head of Brooke, just Karisma. So it's hard to say."

"I think Brooke is perfect," he says. "But if she was a mannequin, just think of all the Prismacolor pencils you'd go through doing her eyebrows."

So he *was* listening when I told him how a mannequin's eyebrows are drawn.

"Thousands," I say.

I collapse against the brick wall in a fit of giggles. He joins me. Our heads arc close together. X-It's face swims before me, isolated by the electric and bracing October night. His breath brushes my cheek. Our lips circle each other more than once.

And never manage to connect.

CHAPTER THREE

New York
November, 1980

The candles flicker, cozy and eerie, held firm by fiberglass hands. Inspired by Jean Cocteau's immortal film *La Belle et La Bête*—another film festival attended at X-It's insistence—I acquired eight mannequin arms from work. I painted them white, screwed them to the wall, and now stand back to admire the effect of my new wall sconces, four on each side of the non-working fireplace. I also painted monochromatic faces on the mantle, and decry my inability to make the eyes follow me everywhere in the room.

Satisfied, I drape myself over the decrepit chaise lounge X-It and I rescued from the curb three blocks south of our apartment. I positioned the chaise at an angle in the center of the large room. Swaths of gauze make it, if not elegant, at least usable.

The hair stands up on the back of my neck.

"You're done, then."

X-It materializes behind me.

I sit up. "I'd like to add some ivy trailing around, and maybe a rug."

"No rug."

"Why not?" I swivel my neck to look up at him.

"Would ruin it." He rolls his shoulders, a peculiar mannerism that isn't quite a shrug and is almost a shudder. "We should go. It's not cool to arrive too fashionably late to your own party," he says.

"It's not my party," I insist.

"It's your artwork. You're not wearing that are you?" He rolls his shoulders again at my army flapper uniform. "Come in my room."

Dance-o-Matic, a nightclub in the Chelsea district, agreed to hang my latest series. My only series ever completed, in fact. I usually find a way of talking myself out of finishing anything worthwhile.

The inspiration for the paintings came from an overdue library book that traveled to New York with me because I was too ashamed to return it. The book is a collection of photographs taken of Victorian cemetery art.

I painted portraits of deceased rock and roll icons depicted as graveyard sculptures. Elvis, Jim Morrison, Janis Joplin etc. I was able to talk—well, X-It did the talking— the Dance-o-Matic assistant manager into hanging the paintings because I used blacklight paint on black board and it fit in with their promotional Blacklight Night.

"Let me dress you," X-It says.

"What?"

He tears open his latest sketchbook. "I want to make you look like this."

"Hmm. I don't know," I say, looking over the drawings. Yet I yearn to be his Karisma, to make him happy, to be his. "All right."

Half an hour later, I get into a taxi, an unheard of expense attributed to X-It's care, not for me although I'm half naked, but for his masterpiece. Tonight we debut our arts together.

I endure the stares in the long line outside Dance-o-Matic.

Annoyed, X-It says, "Go up there and tell them you're the artist."

"I don't like that game."

"Game?"

"The get in free because of who you are or who you know game."

"What are you doing in New York? You might not get in at all if you leave it up to the doorman." He scans the crowd loitering around the club entrance.

"Shouldn't your masterpiece guarantee my entry?" I shiver.

He glares at me. I stare back at the black Andy Warhol turtleneck that is his uniform, then I give in and edge up to the front. The dragon at the gate takes the form of a thick-necked bouncer in Adam Ant get-up. I imagine he applied the feathers as bait for a brawl.

"I'm J.J. Buckingham," I stammer. "My paintings are on your walls."

"Your tits are on my mind," says the man sporting war paint. "They're standing straight up. What are those?" He points to my chest. "Dishwashing gloves?"

"Can I get in?"

"Are you on the guest list?"

"I don't know." I watch X-It strike up a conversation with a middle-aged vampira standing just inside. I tell the bouncer my name and he runs his finger down the clipboard.

"Nope. Tell ya what. I'll let you pay me instead of going back to the end of the line."

I pull a small wad of bills out of the bikini top X-It did indeed fashion for me out of split-apart yellow dishwashing gloves. As I straighten my mini-skirt he constructed from a black Raiders tee shirt, X-It smiles at me as he is escorted inside for free by the bloodsucker in black.

Dance-o-Matic comprises four floors, the higher you go the more exclusive they become. I've only ever been on the first two. My paintings hang on the walls of the main dance area on the ground floor, hard to see beyond the bodies writhing and pulsating beneath the strobes and blacklights. I detest new wave dance music, yet seem to spend a good deal of time dancing to it here at Dance-o-Matic, at Mudd Club, or at the Sphinx in my neighborhood.

Relentless rhythm and beat pull me out amongst the gyrating bodies. It no longer matters that X-It is nowhere to be seen. My body demands to dance. Elvis and Janis gaze stonily at me from their elegant sepulchers. The tiny gear that is J.J. Buckingham finally meshes with the larger mechanism of the world and turns around, cogs connected and efforts effectual.

I throw my arms over my head and spin as the mirror ball splashes color onto the walls and my paintings. My eyelids flutter shut, and I can't stop a smile from ruining the cool of my face.

Four songs later, I require a drink. As I make my way to the bar, I notice the blonde laden with crucifixes who dances in front of the DJ's booth every night, begging him to play her demo tape. That girl needs to get a life. She is omnipresent in bustier and black mesh gloves.

I remember that the downstairs bar is built to be so tall I can barely peer over it. I'll never get served. Upstairs I go.

There's still no sign of X-It. His social climbing has taken him above my level. All of a sudden I feel foolish wearing his rags. Two men walk down the stairwell and glance at me in appreciation. I recognize one guy as the club assistant manager. He halts mid-step and jabs a finger at nothing in particular.

"Hey, you're the blacklight Elvis painter. Right?"

I see only the details of his dress, Rockabilly hair, bolo tie and black-and-white pointy cowhide shoes, known as creepers. "Yes."

"You managed to give him a little class."

"Oh."

He stands one stair above me and appears distracted by my cleavage. "Would you like to come up to the third floor and have a drink with us? We were just headed that way."

As they had been coming down the stairwell, I let that go with nothing more than a raised eyebrow and offer my arm for escort. The third floor. Tonight's my night!

Half an hour later, the assistant manager and his friend remove to the bar, searching for less insecure pastures. In the neo-retro Naugahyde booth, I move the swizzle stick up and down against the side of my plastic drink cup. I know it must be squeaking, but I can't hear it above the thumping music.

X-It slides in next to me.

"Oh, hello." I don't let on I'm aggravated with him. "I was just thinking of going back downstairs."

"Don't! You won't get up here again. I'm quite proud of you, you know. Are you going to date the assistant manager?"

I strain to hear a note of jealousy, but his voice is all friendliness.

"He doesn't want a date." I take a sip. "Are you going to sleep with the Bloodsucker in Black?"

"Who?"

"The woman you came in with."

He puckers and says, "I'm not going to sleep with anyone unless they're famous."

"Does that mean you're a vir—?"

X-it stands in the booth and waves his arms. "Jason! Over here!"

A lithe young man, eyes hidden by the sheepdog bangs of an Echo and the Bunnymen haircut, makes his way to the table.

"J.J.," X-It commands. "Stand up. Walk over there and back. Like a model on a runway. And do the turn thing."

What the heck. I've had just enough vodka and grapefruit juice to give it a try. I squelch the small part of me that wants to slap his face. I square my shoulders.

I sense all movement in the room stop as I make my way down and back across the imaginary catwalk. All eyes are on me. I relax and add a sensuous look over my shoulder as I pivot and stride back to the table.

Local applause bursts forth briefly and dies. I stand, feeling stupid.

X-It and Jason are deep in discussion over my outfit.

"—you should intern on Seventh Avenue. Make calls. Show them your portfolio. Your stuff's hot," says the sheepdog.

X-It looks down, withdrawn. "Just wanted to show it to you."

Ahem. I say, "I think I'll go downstairs now."

They both turn to look at me as if I'm a mannequin come to life.

"Nice moves," says the sheepdog. "Too bad you're not two feet taller." He turns back to X-It. "Come up to the fourth floor with me, there's someone I want you to meet."

X-It gives me a conspiratorial wink, as if I should be happy that he is rising to the fourth floor and not inviting me along.

Crestfallen, I adjust the dishwashing gloves as I thread my way down the crowded stairs. Those that cannot gain admittance to the third floor swarm there like hopeful sperm waiting for their big chance to enter the overrated ovum.

The dark entrance to the second floor beckons to me. Inside, the haunting strains of *Bela Lugosi's Dead* by Bauhaus have driven all new wave giddiness from the room. The DJ is not much older than me. His shoulder length black hair swings back and forth beneath a battered top hat.

With some of my shyness sandpapered away by humiliation and hurt, I walk up to the DJ booth. "Can you play any Sleepers?"

His eyes flick up, then down again. "You're a Raiders fan. I don't take requests from Raiders fans."

"Would a fan allow someone to do this to her tee shirt?"

A smile breaks on his face. "You've got a point. You like The Sleepers? You, my wee lassie, must be from San Francisco."

"Yes. But I live here now, in Alphabet City."

"Careful going home, then, in that get-up. I don't have their EP here in the booth. It's in my bag in the employee room. Stay here and watch this."

The Third floor *and* a stint in the DJ's booth. Having your paintings hanging on the walls of a club brings you magical powers. If only X-It would spend some time with me. Only me.

The DJ returns and plays The Sleepers along with other dirge-like music the Second Floor crowd appreciates. I dance in a near trance.

The assistant manager in bolo tie and cowhide appears and demands the DJ put on *I Am A Poseur* by X-Ray Spex.

As I flee, X-It meets me at the door, his face radiant. "Look who Jason introduced me to. She's gorgeous. She's tall. She can wear my clothes and look like a model."

I swing around prepared to see no less than Karisma at X-It's side, but it is much worse.

I gasp out, "Penny?"

"Hi J.J." says my copper-haired nightmare. "Bet you didn't expect to see me, huh? Hey, you're outfit's kinda cool. I've been in town a couple of days. My friends came too. You know, like they always do."

The floor buckles and I'm not even on drugs. This is the worst possible news. Her friends came too? She's been in town a couple of days and has already made it to the fourth floor of Dance-o-Matic? How like Penny. I want to vomit.

Penny keeps talking, "Something's happening downstairs. X-It said we should find you and go check it out."

X-It rubs my bare shoulder, sending unexpected warm tingles down my legs. At least he thought of me.

"Oh. Okay," I say, stunned. "Who else is here?"

Penny smiles with her too-big, too-white teeth. "The usual gang."

The usual gang I moved far, far away from. I grip the stair rail.

X-It's lips—the lips I consider mine—form a pout. "You know each other?"

"From Frisco," I say glumly.

"San Francisco," corrects Penny, then she whirls to canter her long legs down the stairs.

This cannot be happening. The people I ran away from are invading my New York.

X-It takes my elbow. "Pretend you're Audrey Hepburn in My Fair Lady and you're walking into the Royal Ball as my creation."

I yank my arm away. "Why don't you pretend to be my friend and come downstairs and see my paintings with me?"

"You are my friend, J.J. My best friend. Nobody understands like you do."

An irrational dread twines around my heart. If Penny and her gang can steal my New York, they can take X-It away from me too.

"Understands what?" I ask.

"The way you point out in the morning that the color of eggs beaten with milk is one of the prettiest colors in the world. Or when I spilled the big bag of M&M's on the floor, you wouldn't let me clean it up for awhile because it was so beautiful. You're beautiful."

I take his elbow.

Downstairs in the main dance area, a local East Village band I like, Generika, is on stage. No one is paying the band's distinctive bass licks much notice.

I step into the large room and gape in incomprehension.

Penny runs past me, chortling, and presses an object into my hands. Blacklight paint. Club patrons are smearing bottles of the stuff on themselves, the furniture, each other, and my paintings.

"Noooo!" I cry.

Penny bounces back towards me as glowing idiots begin to tear and shred my artwork from the walls. The pieces float like snowflakes in the strobes and blacklights and then come to rest on the floor, where dancers dance upon the graves of Jim, Jimi, and Janis.

"What's the matter? Join in! You haven't become a serious New Yorker, have you?" Penny manages to appear striking smeared in blacklight paint. "You're not worried about the paintings, are you? They're just kitschy crap the club put up."

I'm on my way out the door.

X-It stops me. "If you know all these people, the least you could do is introduce me." He gestures to the group around Penny.

No screams inside me head. But I whirl to face Penny and her entourage.

I take a breath. "X-It, this is Crikey, Pyro, Dogbite, and the Mod Sisters. Penny, you've already met. I need to go home now." I bite my tongue to keep from crying.

Crikey bursts forth in his Australian accent, "Wow, missy, took a bit a nerve to walk out the door wearing that."

I don't respond. I'm almost to the freedom of the cold city night. A coat falls around my shoulders. I turn to see the assistant manager's cowhide shoes walking away. I pull his coat tight. The last thing I hear, before street noises drown out those of the club, is X-It's voice crowing, "And she couldn't get in for free, so she paid seven dollars for people to see her in it!"

CHAPTER FOUR

I run. I excel at running. Blinded by betrayal, I sprint left instead of right. Blocks later, the shut-tight metal doors of the Chelsea meatpacking district surround me before I'm aware that I've turned the wrong direction. Blood smell rises from the dark sidewalk surface.

A half naked bird should fly home to its nest. Some homing instinct.

I stop to regain my breath. The cold air catches up to me and I shudder. Hands on knees, my ribcage heaves, my heart slows. The magnitude of standing alone in Manhattan at one a.m. strikes me with full force. I pull three dollars from my dishwashing bra, not enough for a cab. Shit, if I hadn't bought a drink I'd have enough. I can't attempt to walk home. I might be stopped by a police officer, or worse.

My instinct says to hide. I creep from loading dock to loading dock, still heading east, away from my apartment. Panic, not peace, accompanies the growing cold.

Headlights turn the corner, followed by the hissing of tires on wet asphalt. I slip inside the crack between two warehouses. The car glides past. I imagine its occupants to be warm, stylishly dressed, and on their way to a top secret after-hours party. I dare not jump out and ask for help. The people in the car could just as easily be creatures of the night a young woman should avoid.

My nose tells me the water's edge is close.

Small red reflections blink in succession on a drenched section of pavement. Blink, blink, blink. I raise my gaze to look down the street and out over the river.

Good To The Last Drop. Drop. Drop.

The giant Maxwell House coffee cup across the waterway continues to drip never ending drops of neon comfort into the water, which, ironically, is coffee-colored in the daylight. In the dark, I can make out the shadowy shapes of pier pilings.

By instinct I've come to my and X-It's special place.

I creep out onto the decaying jetty with extreme care. Treacherous by day, at night the black sucking holes between timbers threaten death. Upon reaching the end, I sit hugging my knees. The gurgling of the river beneath me as it eats away the wood pilings becomes the sound of coffee percolating, warm, steaming, and good to the last drop.

My cold and hungry imagination clings to the aroma of coffee brewing, each hissing drop speaks of orderly domestic mornings, couples going to work, mothers packing lunches.

The neon coffee cup and city lights dance on the surface of the water. So pretty. Yet, it seems as though every time I reach for something beautiful, something exciting, something good, it is torn apart like my paintings, kicks me in the teeth like X-It, or has an accident and is smashed beyond recognition like my father. Maybe all the beautiful aspects of life I crave are simply reflections of a more heavenly plane I'm barred from.

I shift on the pier. The gurgling of the river underneath changes from percolating coffee to the death rattle of a drowned person.

The tears I'd suppressed in the club fall freely.

Even at this hour, barges move on the river. Their horns low like distant cattle. I pull the sides of the men's sport jacket together and lay my head on my knees. As night progresses toward dawn, traffic on the water increases, mirroring that of Manhattan streets as the "city that never sleeps" wakes up. I drift off.

"Here you are!"

I startle and turn to look.

X-It traverses the gaps and sunken timbers of the rotting pier with nonchalance. He has the foresight to bring me a coat, his bicycle messenger's rain poncho. He glances at the assistant manager's jacket I wear, then stuffs the rainproof poncho over my head and sits down next to me. With sounds of plastic crinkling, our bodies touch from hip to shoulder, reminding me how fit he is.

"Missed you when I got home," he says without looking at me.

I pull the slicker down around me and force my frozen mouth to try and speak. My garbled emotions swing from the sting of embarrassment, to his betrayal, to relief and joy at the sight of him. Silent, I gape like a trout.

He turns his ethereal eyes, set too wide apart in his face, to stare into mine. A smile tugs at his lips. He takes my hands as though he's an enthusiastic toddler reaching for his favorite babysitter.

"I've got to tell you what happened after you left. Penny got us into this great after party in Soho. You shoulda been there. There were girls walking around covered only in clay!"

I shift slightly away from him. "G-g-glad to hear somebody wore l-less than I did last night."

He fails to notice the bitter edge to my voice, hidden as it is behind cold stutters, and continues as if nothing between us has changed.

"I want to own a club where I have stuff like that, he says. "You know, I could have it in a basement with a curving stairwell. The wall of the stairwell would be clear acrylic, and girls covered in paint would descend alongside patrons as they come in. The paint would smear. It'd be great."

I think only of the mess and clean up involved. As his angelic child's face beams at me, I realize I can't chastise him for last night. It'd be like yelling at a puppy for peeing on the floor. I need to show him the newspaper.

"I really care for you, X-It."

"Really?"

"Very much.

He puts his arm around me. "Remember the last time we came out here and talked 'til dawn?"

The warmth from his arm and torso revives me. My appetite wakes up.

"Yeah," I say. "We had breakfast afterward at the Polish restaurant on Second Avenue. Want to go there now?"

"They're not open, yet." He cuddles even closer. "Tell me about Penny and her gang. How do you know her? She's really charismatic. She should front a band."

"She can't sing." I stuff my jealousy by reminding myself he *had* gone to the trouble of finding me. "Penny is the forgotten first daughter of a Hollywood television hairdresser and the woman who owns the Le Pierrot chain of gift stores in California."

I think X-It will be impressed with those family stats, but he appears unfazed. He says, "What do you mean 'forgotten'?"

"Her parents divorced, remarried, and have small children. Penny's a reminder to them. Not a welcome one."

"That's sad."

"Don't feel too sorry for her." I sniff as my warming nose begins to drip.

X-It nods. "I suppose not, because she told me she's starting at Parsons in January. That's why she's here. Her parents are footing the whole bill. She even gets an allowance."

"Parsons?" I'm shaken. I want more than anything to go to art school. When Penny reaches for the glitter, she gets gold.

"Yeah, she said Parsons." X-It moves to sit on his heels and bounces with excitement. "Who are the other people? Her entourage? I mean, who moves across country because their friend is going to college? Why do they follow her around?"

I grit my teeth. Coming to New York was MY idea first. "Why did you follow her around Dance-o-Matic and all over Soho?" I hug my knees tighter.

"You didn't follow her. She followed you to New York." X-It looks proud, but he avoids my question.

"Well, I didn't invite her here. I like having New York, and you, for myself." I wait tensely for his reaction.

He punches me on the arm. "New York's a big place."

Not the reaction I yearn for. I shrug. "Hope it's big enough." A sudden chill shakes me. Penny didn't mention Voodoo.

"X," I say, "There's somebody else I tried to leave behind. He's not good—"

"So what about the others," X-It interrupts. "Who's Crikey?"

I'm happy to put off talking about Voodoo. "Crikey's from Australia. Somehow that makes him cool, because of his sort-of British accent." I look skyward. "He used to date Penny."

"He's good-looking enough."

"Oh yes, very GQ. And really, he's a nice guy. Interesting. He rode his motorcycle from one end of Australia to the other. And he's shrimped in Belize. I thought he was headed for Nepal when I left San Francisco. Penny said she dumped him because his equipment was, well, substandard."

X-It actually blushes. I've never seen that before. "And he still follows her around?"

"Maybe New York's a stopover on his way to Nepal?" I answer.

"How about the others?"

Why couldn't he just let them drop? "They're a tight knit group. Their claim to fame is being punk right since the beginning. From the Zebra Club in San Diego, to The Whiskey a Go-Go in LA, to the Mabuhay Gardens in San Francisco. They were there."

"Huh, like I was in D.C."

I send my gaze skyward again. I detest punks who play the "who's cooler than who" game. It defeats the whole point of being losers.

I sigh. "Dogbite and Pyro are brother and sister." I give X-It an up-and-down sidelong glance. "And they're not going to like you."

"Why?" X-It looks shocked at the thought.

"Because you care. About Art. About Beauty. Pyro and Dogbite would just as soon swallow gasoline, take a flammable piss on everything then toss a lit match."

"They'd be famous for fifteen minutes." He smiles.

"What?"

"Andy Warhol's brilliant prophecy. He says in the future everyone will be famous for fifteen minutes. Just wait, it'll be his most important contribution to Art."

Remembering what he said in the club last night about not sleeping with anyone unless they were famous, I remark, "If everyone's famous it will improve your love life."

X-It frowns at me. I fervently wish he'll talk about it. Why can't he see how much I love him?

"Who are the Mod sisters?" he asks.

My patience ebbs away, but I answer him because he's X-It. "They're not really sisters. Just two girls who live their lives as if Quadrophenia is playing inside their heads. Which accounts for the Merton parkas, sixties clothes, Jam albums, and the fact they'll sleep with anyone who owns a Vespa."

Voodoo's face appears suddenly in my mind. "X-It, there's someone else in Penny's group, who wasn't at the club last night—"

"If they weren't there, they're not important." He looks at his watch. "Polish restaurant's open. Let's go. My bike's at the beginning of the pier. I'll walk it."

I stand, unfolding shaky heron legs, and pull out my three dollars, warm from my breasts. "Here's what I got."

He shakes his head as if I'm the neophyte. "You should have tried harder to get in free. I'll spot you."

But he knew exactly where to find me. I accept his outstretched hand.

Even in the East Village I collect stares as I walk beside X-It on St. Mark's Place, my thin bare legs sticking out beneath the poncho like the handle of a giant, storm-battered umbrella. We turn on Second Avenue and then into the steamy third world of the Polish coffee shop.

Once seated and served, I stare down at the pillow of blueberry pancakes on my plate and force my cold stiff fingers to move the fork. Voodoo can't be here. Penny would've said.

"X-It, there's always been another member of Penny's gang. Someone evil."

X-It's head snaps up. "Nobody's evil."

"Voodoo is. He works hard at it."

"Aw, come on. Penny says you don't like her, and it's hard to believe how anyone could not like Penny."

I wrinkle my nose. X-It is in actual danger of becoming another mindless asteroid in Penny's orbit. Damn her and the airplane ticket that brought her here.

He continues, "If this Voodoo guy is a friend of Penny's, he can't be that bad."

"You don't know what you're saying. I hope he stayed in California." Where Penny should have. Where they all should have. New York and X-It belong to me.

As we leave the restaurant, drizzle wets the sidewalks and begins to sheet on my poncho. A vague satisfaction in knowing my outfit now makes sense settles over me and somehow redeems the night before. Framed by the blinkers of my plastic hood, my apartment building's front door comes into view.

I hold the door for X-It and his pony express bike. He stands dripping on the tiny hexagonal white tiles of the entryway as I search for my keys. I drop them. They clatter on the tile and skitter against the doorjamb. I stoop to retrieve the keys, careful to bend my knees in the absurd Raiders mini skirt.

An object that shouldn't be there catches my eye. Stuck to the lower part of the door with a heavy stickpin is a small figure made of black yarn and wire. I jump back and drop the keys again.

"He's here."

The figure resembles a tiny Guatemalan Trouble Doll; only those are colorful and intended to take away the recipient's troubles. This foreboding little stick person brings with it a big black cloud.

"Who's here?"

"Voodoo." I point to the yarn effigy.

X-It reaches toward it.

"Don't touch it!"

X-It pulls the figure from the door, examines it, and then sticks it in his pocket. "It's cool."

I rub my forehead and enter the apartment. All is quiet and serene. Except for my heart. How did Voodoo find me? For X-It's sake, I play it cool and don't discuss Voodoo or his menacing calling card. I look around my apartment but all is as it should be.

Neither I nor X-It have to work today, Sunday. In the bathroom, I shower warmth back into my limbs. I wish X-It would join me, even if it's only to warm up. No such luck. I return to my room wrapped only in a towel and stand before the dark fireplace.

The floor creaks with soft footsteps. Warm breath brushes my moist skin. X-It stands behind me. Will he wrap his arms around me? I will him to do so. The second I take to make that wish is long enough for him to flee the room. I whirl to face emptiness.

The mannequin arms on my wall reach out to me. They beckon me to bed, offering cold caresses for my disappointment. I collapse on my chaise lounge, pulling up the blankets. Sleep creeps along the edges of my thoughts. I try not to think of the doll on the door, or what it means.

Voices come from X-It's room. He always falls asleep to his wideband radio, continually switching from station to station, blending fragmented words, languages, and sentences into a chance reality with meaning all his own.

The radio's multiple personalities transmute into a soundtrack—an incoherent Greek chorus of strange significance—to my dreams.

CHAPTER FIVE

The same layered cacophony of voices who escorted me into sleep prod me into wakefulness. Afternoon sun begins to fade behind the tall shuttered windows as I sit up on the chaise lounge. My ears sort through the voices and other stirring sounds that shouldn't be there. These noises aren't coming from X-It's wideband radio. People are in my apartment.

I scuttle to where I keep my clothes in a corner of my room then dash on an outfit consisting of a forties gabardine shirt buttoned up to the neck, suspenders, and Zoot pants.

"Aw, don't cover that up, I was enjoying myself." The voice purrs at me, an almost-drawl from behind the beaded curtain that separates my room from the rest of the apartment.

A dark hand beset with many rings and bracelets parts the strands of beads and makes its way into the room, bringing its owner with it.

"J.J." Hands extend. Bracelets jingle. "Give me a hug."

I walk numbly across the room and give Voodoo his required embrace.

"Nice room." He does a carousel twirl on one booted heel to take in my abode. "Very cool."

"How'd you find my apartment?"

He cocks one eyebrow. His hair is short in back, but in front his black curls tumble down to his wicked Romany smile. His wry expression chastises me for having to ask.

A point-down pentacle glimmers on his chest, nestled amid curling hair as dark and ominous as a fairy-tale forest.

"Why are you here at all?"

"You have to ask? This is New York!" He sticks his head out through the beads. "Hey, everybody, J.J.'s awake. You have got to come see this room."

He holds aside the beaded curtain and Pyro, Dogbite, the Mod Sisters, Crikey, Penny, and last of all, X-It, parade into the sanctuary of my soul. Penny starts to flip through my paintings stacked in the corner. Dogbite reaches to shake a mannequin hand.

"Stop it!" I yell.

"Someone woke up cranky." Penny casts a mollifying, heartbreakingly beautiful smile at me.

I am immune.

"This one's not bad." Penny points to a painting of a white rabbit I painted as an homage to the band The Damned.

Penny should talk. Art school isn't going to help her. She draws less well than she sings.

"This one's not bad either," says Voodoo with evident admiration for X-It's person. "Where'd you find him?"

He runs his hand up and down X-It's back. My friend reacts with alarm and hides behind the Mod Sisters. Voodoo laughs, his deep, Halloween, creep show laugh.

Crikey, however, appears bored with the exchange. He informs the group he's heading up to Forty-second Street to hang out for a while and will catch up with the group later, at the Sphinx. He ducks through the beaded curtain. A heartbeat later, the door to the apartment shuts with a bang. The Mod Sisters decide to go vintage clothes shopping and follow him. More rattled beads. Another bang.

Penny bounces on my lounge. "Forty-second Street, who does he think he's kidding?" She snorts and turns to me to explain. "Crikey has decided he's gay. He's gone to check out the male prostitutes for clues on how to look homosexual." She throws her head back. "Don't you know it's so much more cool to be gay?"

"I think you might be taking this personally, Beautiful." Voodoo slides over to Penny, cups her jaw in his hand, and gives her an explicit tongue-twisting kiss. "He never was man enough for you."

Penny pulls back, flushed, her eyes bright.

"Don't you dare try that with me," says Pyro, as if her shaved head with flame tattoos on her scalp isn't enough warning.

"I prefer to kiss your brother."

"Fuckin' faggot," says Dogbite.

Voodoo winks at me, for only I know that macho, mohawked Dogbite is already an old oral conquest of Voodoo's. I want them all out of my house.

Voodoo returns his attention to Penny. "Perhaps I should demonstrate to Crikey that being gay is more than a matter of tight jeans or eyeliner. What do you think, my dear?"

Penny bites her lip. "Is Crikey 'man enough' for you, Voodoo?"

"A morsel. A diversion, certainly. It's so much fun to deflower a straight. Jealous?" Oddly, Penny looks as though she might be.

This conversation reminds me of why I ran away from these people. Ugh. My sudden nausea tells me it's been a long while since I've eaten anything. This group is hard to take on an empty stomach. And here they are, dominating my room and threatening my happiness again.

X-It's voice pipes from the corner as he addresses Voodoo for the first time, "Are you gay?"

"I defy description." Voodoo laughs again. "I think that question is better directed at yourself. Don't you?"

Double ugh. Voodoo hasn't changed. Then his words sink in. I never considered X-It might be gay.

How can Voodoo, someone who oozes all the appeal of a garden snail, which is, by the way, a hermaphroditic creature, see something so clearly that I don't see? That X-It himself doesn't see? No. No way. X-It is not gay.

I glance at X-It. His eyes stretch round with fear. Suddenly socially uncertain of himself, he rolls his shoulders. In a heartbeat I know it doesn't matter. Who cares about the defining terms of a relationship if two souls, stamped at birth with the same spiritual zip code, feel safest residing together? I meet his eyes and smile, a pure, no-strings-attached grin.

X-It walks across the room and takes my hand. My heart soars. He is my best friend, and I will protect him from Voodoo with teeth and claws. He is mine and he is not gay.

"So," I say, swinging X-It's hand. "To what do I owe the honor of having all of you in my apartment?"

"It's X-It's apartment too. Isn't it?" asks Penny.

"My name's on the lease. X-It is my roommate."

Penny looks uncomfortable for just a second. "I'm looking for a place large enough for the whole gang, 'til then I figured we could all stay here."

I find some backbone. "Who told you you could?"

"I did," says X-It. "Your friends are like people out of a movie."

I drop his hand. He drifts a few paces away. Panic seizes me. X-it embodies my family, all my waking moments, my future. What about our art co-op, what about the damn popsicle cart? I can't lose him, not to these freaks from my past.

I watch in frozen horror as X-It's hand decides to place itself into Penny's. He then pries her away from Voodoo's seductive gaze. Silently, he tows Penny into the private bay that is his room and shuts the door. I blink back tears, forget to breathe.

"Hey, Pyro," says Dogbite. "Let's you and me go down to Soho and look for that Cockney Rejects import you wanted." Pyro nods. Dogbite won't look at Voodoo, but grunts good-bye to me.

On his way out of the beaded curtain, a few beads catch on the spikes of his mohawk and jerk his head backward. Angry, he grabs handfuls of slithering strands and yanks the entire curtain off the door lintel.

"God Damn!" He throws it on the floor. Beads bounce, scatter and roll. Brother and sister leave the apartment. That's two more down, for a while at least.

"Temper. Temper," purrs Voodoo. He sashays his narrow hips over to me, his black boots resounding on the floor like a fearsome flamenco dancer. He pins me in the corner. As he bears down on me, I swear his irises are swirling around his pupils. My panic turns to fury and then back to fear.

He pulls at my shirt. "You're so proper, so repressed. J.J. the Type A punk rocker." He snaps my suspenders.

"Ow!" That hurts.

"Women shouldn't wear suspenders." His hand makes its way under my shirt.

I stare stonily at him. Voodoo is the one guy in California I did turn down and he can't stand it. He runs a thumb over my nipple and I shiver. It's the air.

Giggles and shrieks come from X-It's room.

He continues the stroking. "What do you think X-It and Penny are doing in his bedroom with the door shut?"

"I know what they're doing." And I am quite certain I do know for sure.

"So do I. He's proving to himself I'm wrong about him."

I laugh in his face. The predator's spell over his prey is broken. Voodoo's hand returns to his side.

"He's dressing her." I glare at him. "Like a doll. Nothing more."

"Are you willing to bet on that?"

I'm more upset that X-It might be turning Penny into his ideal than I will be if they're mating like rabbits. "Yeah. I'll make a bet." What will Voodoo want? Something so cliché as my soul?

"If I'm right," says Voodoo, "I get to stay in this room while I'm here, with you. What do you want if you're right, although you've little chance?"

"X-It's off-limits to you."

His lower lip comes out. "Done." But he smiles in a way that makes me uneasy.

"Shall we knock?" I say as we cross the apartment.

"I never knock." He swings open the door.

Voodoo and I gasp in unison. Penny is transformed. A co-opted hip-hop/new wave, Japanese runway goddess stands before us.

X-It beams. "I can't wait for people to see her. I wish we were going to a bigger club than Sphinx tonight."

"We can start there," assures Penny. "Then we'll head Uptown."

Voodoo's talons seize my shoulder. He is a sore loser. "How did you know they weren't having sex?"

I grin for the first time since he showed up. "Because Penny's not famous."

Voodoo appears to chew on that for a moment, but X-It says, "Not famous yet."

The phone rings. Sullen in my victory, numb with loss, I answer it.

It's Russ, the Dance-o-Matic assistant manager, calling to tell me he's sorry about what happened to my paintings, and then he offers to take me out to dinner in apology. I glance toward X-It's room. The last thing I want to be part of tonight is Penny's admiring throng. I agree to dinner.

When Russ arrives to pick me up, Penny's entourage has returned to the nest and is in full feather, ready to go clubbing.

I wear my flapper dress, this time with a pair of pumps. As I let my date in the door, Voodoo stands guard, possessive and darkly paternal. I will never understand him and don't want to. Ignoring Voodoo, I grab Russ's hand, maneuver him through the reinstalled, tattered bead curtain and into my room.

He stops dead.

"That's my couch!" He guffaws and slicks back his swoop of hair. "I put it out on the street months ago."

"Already, we have something in common," I say.

Russ nods like a Rockabilly bobble head as he looks about the room. "Hey, this is that building that's haunted."

He has my attention. "What?"

"Yeah, this famous old hippy witch lived here in the sixties. I read about it. When Rosemary's Baby hit the theaters, the neighbors all tried to force her out and failed. She's supposed to haunt the place."

"That's not mentioned in the lease," I say and Russ snorts.

Spying from the other side of the beads, Voodoo says, "Fierce shoes."

He refers to Russ's creepers. I push him aside to escape back through the beads and out the front door with my date. "They're cowhide. Fierce animals, those cows."

Voodoo smiles, but his eyes declare war. As he shuts the apartment door, his eye remains visible in the crack until the last possible moment. The click of the door as it closes in my face angers me like nothing else so far today. This is my apartment.

I forgot to say good-bye to X-It. He doesn't even know I'm going out. Never mind. He's busy. He won't care. I clutch the assistant manager's elbow as I hesitate and consequently miss a step.

"Is something wrong?"

"No."

"Good." He smiles down at me. "Interesting people in your apartment."

I march down Fifth Street. "They're not staying long."

CHAPTER SIX

I share a nice dinner, pleasant company, and absolutely no chemistry with the Dance-o-Matic assistant manager. So I know I'll sleep with him. The proclamation I made on my first night in New York is losing ground, shaken by the invasion of Penny and The Pets.

I invite Russ back to my apartment by saying I will return his sport jacket, which is a good deal more dignified than the one he wears this evening, green and black stripes over a purple tee shirt, over black stovepipe jeans, over the pointy cowhide shoes. I spent the evening with a new wave superhero.

I light the candles held by every fiberglass arm and wish I'd never painted eyes on my fireplace mantle.

"You're a really cool chick. And a fox too."

"Thanks." I suppress the derisive laugh forming in my throat, plop on the lounge, and then kick off my shoes.

Russ wastes no time in settling himself half beside me, half on top of me.

"Look at me, back on my couch." He runs his fingers through his coif, pushes me down to kiss me, then spreads my legs with his hand.

From there it is mere moments until the inevitable. Each of his thrusts drive a nail into the coffin that now houses my dream of a romance with X-It. Nothing can drive away my painful love for him, but each numb and pleasure-less thrust, thrust, thrust, pushes him a little further away.

Russ's breathing grows rapid. As he climaxes, I scream. Voodoo stands on the other side of the beaded curtain, in the darkness of the rest of the apartment, blank-faced, watching me.

From the assistant manager's actions and pleased expression, I guess he thinks I came. How little he knows me. He is now added to my list of terrible and unfulfilling sexual encounters.

Voodoo isn't there.

I jump up and run around the apartment, turning on all the lights and looking in all the closets. No one else is home.

"What's got you spooked?" Russ asks as he zips his jeans.

"I'm not spooked."

"Have it your way. Do you want me to stay?"

"That's okay."

He places a Beta videotape on top of the mantle. "This is for you."

"What is it?"

"Some footage of your paintings, thought you might like to have it. Do you want to go out again?"

"Sure. I had a nice time."

"I'll call you."

"Right."

He leaves.

Now alone with the memory of Voodoo's apparition, I need to call someone. Without X-It, I have no one. I scrape the bottom of the barrel and phone Art Munny back in San Francisco. Each ringing tone calls me a coward.

The phone picks up. "Hello."

"Is Art there?"

"No. He's not home. This is Michael."

"Hi, this is J.J." I breathe a sigh of relief. I didn't really want to talk to Art. Michael's voice sounds so normal.

"J.J.! How's New York?"

I picture him in his Buddy Holly glasses. Michael, I learned at my going away party, is seven years older than me and has already survived a divorce. He possesses a world-weariness which qualifies as wisdom. Before I know it, I've taken a half hour of his time and poured out my entire tale.

"Have you tried asking them to leave?" he reasons.

I wind the telephone cord about my arm. "You don't understand. They're barnacles."

"Barnacles are harmless."

"Well, leeches then." I picture a leech with a mohawk.

"Salt gets rid of leeches."

What the hell does that mean? Is he making fun of me? No one would describe my personality as salty. "I don't know what to do."

"Maybe they won't be there long. Do all of these people live off of Penny's money?"

"I don't know. Voodoo doesn't. He's a drug dealer."

"Sounds like you'd better get him out of your apartment. If your name is on the lease, you can have the police remove everybody."

He makes it sound so rational, so easy. I try to imagine the gumption it would take to bring the police to my apartment.

"Voodoo's scary. He practices black magic."

Michael laughs at me. "And why did you let this guy in the door?"

"I didn't. X-It did. While I was asleep."

"Throw the lot of 'em out."

"I'll try."

"You know," Michael takes a hesitant breath. "It sounds to me like you're a bit jealous of Penny."

"Jealous?"

"Yeah. She's not the only one who can go to art school. Why don't you check it out?"

A small sigh escapes my mouth. "I don't have any money."

"Have you heard of scholarships? Loans?"

"Okay. I'll try." All of a sudden, fatigue pulls at me from every direction.

"Take care of yourself, J.J. You're a diamond in the rough."

A tear forms in the corner of my eye. I cling to his words even though on the surface they are insulting.

"I'll tell Art you called."

"You don't have to." I quickly add, "Michael, can I call you again?"

His voice warms, "Yup. Anytime."

I blow out the candles, lay in the dark, and miss X-It. I rely on our days of work, meals, movie festivals, laundry, and his laughter. He is my heart, my heart now out dancing with someone else. I'll never meet anyone else as cool and original as X-It. I wish he'd just kick me in the gut instead.

Penny claims to be of royal ancestry. I traveled three thousand miles to scrape off her insistent one-upmanship, and her mindless group of asteroids. Like X-It, I once thought them colorful. If her asteroids revolve around Planet Penny, then Penny is in orbit around Voodoo's dark sun, glued fast by the gravity of his blinding teeth, spellbound by the swirling solar flares in his eyes.

I picture X-It trailing behind Penny, a comet of talent in danger of flaming out.

I sit up in sudden fear. Why did I think that? I flop back down. I'm just envious, like Michael said. X-It dances and laughs tonight with others, in places he and I alone cannot enter. I am as miserable as a first grader who must eat lunch alone, or in my case have dinner with a dance club assistant manager.

Unable to cry, I force myself to think of something monumentally awful. *Ronald Reagan is now President of the United States.*

I burst into tears.

At four-thirty in the morning, a key turns in the front door lock. Muzzy from crying and fatigue, I attempt to make out what is going on in my apartment. Boots of all kinds tromp across wood floors. My doorway beads rattle. Bodies flop on pillows and floors. Acrid marijuana smoke drifts across the apartment. The toilet flushes. X-It's radio jumps from station to station, and I surrender to sleep.

* * *

Nine o'clock that evening, I return to my apartment—after a full day at the mannequin factory and four hours at the trendy bakery—to signs of a full day's habitation by the seven unwanted dwarves. X-It caters to them like Snow White. It's enough to make me throw poison apples. I stomp into my room. They've been in here. I know, because the room smells like clove cigarettes, patchouli, and poppers.

X-It comes in behind me. "I missed you last night."

We sit side by side on the lounge. I remain silent.

"Russ phoned while you were at work."

"Who?"

"The Dance-o-Matic guy. So you are going out with him. You had sex with him right here, didn't you?" He looks at me. "Sometimes I think about what sex with you would be like."

I whip my head around but he's off and verbally running away.

"With you dating him, that's cool," he says. "We should form a band. All of us. He could get us gigs there."

The fact that none of us own a musical instrument, let alone possess any proficiency, doesn't stand in the way of X-It's imagination.

"Yeah." I sneer. "You can call yourselves Planet Penny and the Mindless Asteroids."

"Take out the 'mindless,' it's not bad." He takes my hand. "I like Penny. Please let her and her friends stay here? With her parents' money and connections, she'll get her own place really fast."

"Will you move in with her and the gang?"

X-It startles and won't meet my eyes. My damn perceptiveness again.

I can see I've been relegated to the socially useful position of dance club assistant manager's girlfriend, and Penny is X-It's new special friend. I look over at X-It and try to hate him, try to pity him, try to feel emotionally superior, but his nearness, his plea, soaks my heart and I say, "Fine, they can stay, but just until they find a place."

X-It makes his way through the beads giving a thumbs up sign and rejoins the noisy group in the other rooms. I want to hibernate. Maybe when I wake up they'll all be gone and X-It will be mine again. And I dread facing Voodoo after his vicarious peep show last night. Did I imagine him? If so, I don't dare ask my inner workings why he popped up at just that time.

I need defenses. If the Mod Sisters, Crikey, Penny, Pyro, Voodoo, and Dogbite are going to be underfoot for a while, that pretty beaded curtain just will not do.

The following morning, I dress, go shopping for Russian vodka and a chocolate cake, and then ring the doorbell of my downstairs neighbors, the party hearty, jumpsuit-wearing construction boys from Alabama.

The annoyed expressions on their hung over faces quickly turn ecstatic over their salvation. Breakfast is served. A couple of hours later, I turn a key in the deadbolt lock on my new bedroom door. Thick and strong, it has been firmly installed with mysterious and noisy power tools. I decide I will later trim the beads and hang them across the empty fireplace pit as a screen.

Jumpsuit Number One leans seductively against the doorjamb and shakes sawdust out of his blond mullet. "You doin' anything later? I've got vodka left."

Voodoo and X-It suddenly appear on either side of me.

"I've got a boyfriend," I say, thinking of Russ.

My neighbor looks from X-It to Voodoo. "I see." He gathers his power tools and leaves.

Voodoo and X-It survey my massive new door. X-It's face tells me he thinks I am no longer available. I want to reach out, to put my arms around him and tell him that all he has to do is knock and I'm his. But he moves away from me and returns to his room, where he and Penny are experimenting with coating strands of their hair with nail polish. Voodoo's face betrays only the excitement of an added challenge.

CHAPTER SEVEN

New York City
Late November - Early December, 1980

I'm painting on unstretched canvas laid out on the floor of my room. Dissatisfaction with my efforts makes me hungry. I start to head toward the kitchen for a snack and stop when I hear the front door open and the clicking heels of the Mod Sisters cross the floor. Silently, I turn my dead bolt and crack my door ajar, so I can peer out.

As the two girls head for the living room, I note their style has improved since coming to New York. The vintage clothing stores in this city outshine anything San Francisco has to offer, unless one desires to dress as a Haight Street hippie. The Mod Sisters have gone from looking like surfer versions of LuLu in *To Sir With Love*, to sleek and sinister imitations of Marlo Thomas in *That Girl*.

I watch from my room as the girls wilt down onto the floor pillows. Voodoo slides out the far bedroom door and comes towards them.

"Do you have them?" asks Sheila, Mod Sister number one.

"Maybe," answers Voodoo coyly.

"Come on," says Trish, Mod Sister number two. "You said you'd have them. We agreed on the price. We'll need 'em if we're going out tonight."

"Don't worry dearies, you'll be out of your brains on the five-fifteen."

"Whaddya know," snaps Trish, "he's seen the movie."

"Be nice," says Sheila to Trish, and then turns back to Voodoo. "Has to be Dexies or Bennies. We don't touch anything else."

Hah, hah, and hah. I remember a night at the Mabuhay Gardens when the girls made do with chocolate covered espresso beans and diet pills.

"I know. I know," says Voodoo. As a magician produces a bouquet of flowers from thin air, a baggie of blue pills appears in his hands. The baggie comes to a point at the top, secured with a jaunty twist-tie, which makes it look like a big Hershey's Kiss.

Trish moves to grab it.

"Uh, uh, uh. Money first, like always."

Sheila pulls out her wallet and counts out an awful lot of money. How do the Mod Sisters pay for their drugs? I'd rather not know. I shut my door so it doesn't make a sound, and turn the dead bolt.

I clean my paintbrushes then put on my shoes and a coat. Today is Saturday and I'm due at the bakery for an afternoon shift. I choose to forgo a snack until my break at work. The good thing about working at the bakery is the abundance of free things to eat.

I slam the front door on my way out, that method of goodbye being preferable to having to speak to Voodoo. As I head toward Fourteenth Street and the cross-town subway, I pass the laundromat where, until Penny's arrival, X-It and I shared weekly rituals of washing, drying, folding and silliness.

I catch sight of a flaming scalp sitting on the floor in front of the wall of dryers. Pyro. Dogbite sits cross-legged next to her.

I stick my head in the door. The atmosphere of detergent and warm lint contrasts with the bitter cold air outside.

"Hey, Pyro, Dogbite. You doing laundry?"

Neither brother nor sister responds. Both of their heads move in slight simultaneous circles as their eyes follow the dryers around and around and around.

I lean my shoulders through the doorway and shout, "Pyro!"

No reaction. Nothing. Dogbite and Pyro have ventured deep into the land of Nod.

I enter and squat in front of my ersatz roommates. "Where'd you guys get junk from?"

The corner of Pyro's mouth lifts up a trifle. "Voodoo."

"Why are you doing that stuff?" I can feel my face scrunch up. "You guys never did before."

She lifts her face, eyes vacant. "It's New York, stupid."

Dogbite adds, "And Voodoo offered freebies."

The pair return to watching the dryers.

A Russian woman in a shapeless coat and puce headscarf spits on the floor next to the siblings. She lifts her gaze to glare at me.

"You with them?" She throws a wadded dishtowel at me. "Get out of here, junkie."

I shut the door in self-defense and hurry on my way.

All through my shift, I worry about Pyro and Dogbite. These are two people I don't want in my apartment, don't want in my life, and who have only ever shown me a grunting tolerance. But I will pry Voodoo's talons from their flesh with a needle nosed pliers if it will make any difference. But I know they are lost.

My suspicions are confirmed when I come home from work and brother and sister are sprawled, unconscious, on the floor pillows in the living room. Pyro's motorcycle jacket sleeve is pushed up her arm, revealing many red track marks on her pale skin. I marvel at the number. Dogbite and Pyro haven't been in New York City very long.

Sid Vicious sneers at me from the front of Dogbite's tee shirt. I can almost swear he drools onto Dogbite's chest.

"Well, Sid," I speak to the tee shirt, "He'd better not follow in your footsteps in my apartment." I have the immediate guilty thought that an overdose or two would cut down on the number of unwanted dwarves. At least the siblings' growing addiction makes them less aggressive. Much less aggressive.

A movement causes me to turn around. Voodoo leans against the doorjamb. He meets my eyes and grins triumphantly over the bodies on the floor. Sickened, I leave the room.

Russ requested my presence tonight at Dance-o-Matic. He manages the band Generika as well as the nightclub. Tonight he can combine both jobs, as Generika is booked at the club. I wear my now signature style. Tonight's flapper dress is white silk. In the bathroom, I part my hair in the middle and flatten it, pulling a curl forward on either side of my face.

"Wow," says X-It, peeking in, fresh from work and the outside world. "You look like a punk Louise Brooks."

"That'll work." I smile.

"You going to Dance-o-Matic tonight?"

"Yeah, Russ asked me."

"Cool, we're all going too. I've got a special dress for Penny this evening."

I sigh a twofold sigh. The last time I wore one of X-It's creations was a disaster, but I still want to be his model.

I say, "I wouldn't count on Pyro and Dogbite going anywhere."

X-It glances into the living room. "Don't worry. Voodoo'll get them up." I do worry.

Crikey pokes his head in the bathroom door as well. "Beautiful, missy. Any chance a mate can get in there and put on his eyeliner?"

He sidles past X-It. I watch him enter by looking in the mirror. The handsome Australian wears a Chinese silk smoking jacket and tuxedo pants.

"Hold it!" cries X-It, "You two are a still frame out of a silent movie." He boxes the scene with his hands like a movie director.

I laugh. "Go get dressed."

"I am dressed." He points to his work clothes. His bicycle messenger's garb does possess a certain post-apocalyptic, Dickensian flair.

I shrug. "Cool."

Russ asked me to arrive a bit early, so I leave the apartment before anyone else. On my way out, I glance into the living room. Voodoo is propping up Pyro and assisting her in the act of snorting a line of white powder up her nose. Pyro wakes right up. I flee.

I am to meet Russ at the service entrance to Dance-o-Matic. A gentle snow drifts across the streetlights and I glance up at the building.

Band members mill about the back door, blowing warm breath on their hands. Russ recognizes me and nods to the bassist, who sets down his two guitar cases on the lightly powdered ground.

"Evening there, J.J. girl. Good to see ya," says Russ. Snowflakes fall on his head, adding short-lived dandruff to the black Rockabilly swoop. "You can take those in."

He smiles and nods to the cases as if he's granting me the world's largest favor, and then he walks into the club. I halt in my tracks. My eyelids close as I decide what to do. The shushing caress of snowflakes can't dispel the embarrassment burning my cheeks.

That asshole. I blink back tears, swallow my pride, and after everyone else goes inside, pick up the guitars.

Although angry, I'm not above using the social clout of having come in the back door while holding guitars as an entrée to the fourth floor. There, I hide from Russ and drink vodka and grapefruit juice. In a quasi-revolutionary act, the bartender watches Monday Night Football on the television in the corner. She must rate in the Dance-O-Matic universe since the TV is louder than the Talking Heads' song now playing.

At eleven-fifteen, the grating voice of Howard Cosell interrupts the game. His words sound unnatural in connection with football. I look up.

"What did he say?" I lean over to ask the bartender and spill my drink. Towel in hand, the woman moves as if in a trance. Tears pour down her cheeks.

I ask her again, "What did he say?"

Her glazed eyes do not see me. She wipes the bar. "John Lennon's dead," she says. "He's been shot."

CHAPTER EIGHT

New York
Mid-December, 1980

The nonsensical death of a childhood icon makes everything surreal. New York is less New York now, with him gone.

I stroll beside Rockefeller Center, my hands shoved deep in my pockets, as much a gesture of cocooning self-protection as it is to shelter my hands from the cold and wind. The harder my hands press into my pockets, the more my shoulders round in my inadequate thrift store coat, which still carries a trace of an old lady's scent.

The skaters making use of the ice rink below move and twirl in prescribed motion, which mimics miniature figures I've seen under the tree in my grandmother's Christmas village.

Twinkle lights refract in the icy air, reflecting off every shiny urban surface. Salvation Army bell-ringers provide the earnest soundtrack, and smells of roasted chestnuts from the vendor's cart on the corner force deep Currier and Ives longings from my chest. In reaction, I vow to throw a Sex Pistols holiday party.

Then I remember why I'm out roaming mid-town Manhattan in the bitter cold. Voodoo and his drugged marionettes occupy my apartment. Penny monopolizes X-It.

Squeals of bicycle tires sound on the sidewalk. I flinch. After recovering, I look up into X-It's beaming face. He must've jumped the curb when he spotted me. Angry pedestrians curse at him over their shoulders as they hurry home with their Christmas shopping treasures.

"You off work?" I ask. My heart races at the thought of him seeking me out. I try to radiate nonchalance.

"I just have to drop off my route record. Down in the basement over there." He points with a heavily gloved hand.

All about me the yuletide cheer screams for my attention. I crave to take part in the festivities, not as an outsider, not as a girl who carries guitars for jerks.

I bunny hop toward him and grab his handlebars. "Let's ice skate!"

After momentary surprise, he rolls his shoulders and says, "Yeah, sure. Walk with me. I'll drop this off then we can rent skates."

On the ice at Rockefeller center, I hold X-It's elbow and edge along the slippery surface with tentative Frankenstein steps. Why did this seem like a good idea a few minutes ago?

X-It lacks proficiency, but he skates as he does everything else, with fluidity and grace. He smiles down at me. I hug his elbow closer and relax. My strides ease and we begin to glide as a pair along with the other holiday skaters.

I soak in the decorated trees and garlands, the golden Rockefeller Center statue, and the rosy faces around me. I can almost imagine that everything between us is as it used to be, before Penny. I sing along with the canned Christmas music, "We're gliding along with the song of a wintry fairyland."

"You have a nice voice," interrupts X-It. "You should front our band."

The band still exists only in his imagination. I grin, then close my mouth to hum the rest of the tune. All is right again in my universe, I don't even mind the horrified look on an oncoming mother's face as she nearly dislocates her child's shoulder in an attempt to avoid a collision with me, a spiky, purple-haired Christmas elf.

"Are you going anywhere for the Holidays?" X-It asks.

"Where would I go?" I'm happy right here, and I wish this moment would last forever.

"I don't know. Don't you want to go back and visit where you came from?"

"No," I answer truthfully. "How about you? Do you want to visit your parents in Virginia?" He told me about his home on one of our laundry days.

He says, "Want is a strong word, but yeah. If I can dig up the cash."

The tinsel and sentimentality of Rockefeller Center override my better instincts. "My Dad's in Philadelphia," I say.

"I didn't know you had a dad in Philadelphia." He puffs visible cold air. "Where's your mom?"

"Hard to say from one month to another. She sends me postcards." I reach into my rear pants pocket. "This one's from Encinitas. She's been there for a while. It's almost time to go to the atlas again."

"What?"

"After she's all moved in and all the windows have curtains, she doesn't have anything to distract her from herself, so she stands this giant, old, Rand McNally Atlas of the United States on its spine—we've had it since I was little—lets it fall open, and she's calling U-Haul the next day."

I hand X-It the postcard.

"There's a phone number, and a picture," says X-It. "She's pretty, but who's that?"

"Her boyfriend." My mother always glues a photo of herself and her latest live-in lover on the front of her postcards.

"He's got three fingers missing," remarks X-It.

"Let me see that." But even as I grab for the postcard, I don't doubt it. I sigh and explain, "My mother's last boyfriend had a prosthetic leg. The one before that, a harelip."

I don't tell X-It that my mother dates a string of men with missing parts in an attempt to escape the burdensome memory of the man she loved and married, a man now missing a working brain.

My eccentric mother doesn't faze X-It. He rolls his shoulders as I put the card back in my pocket.

"You know," he says, "I don't even know what J.J. stands for."

I jerk on the ice. The very first week he was my roommate, I found out X-It's real name is Thomas Leavitt, and that he was adopted.

"So?" His eyes search mine.

"Sew buttons on my undies?" I laugh teasingly, let go of his arm, and skate ahead solo.

He catches up, his eyes narrow, and he grabs both of my bare hands with his gloved ones.

"So what does 'J.J.' stand for?"

I bite my lip and stop when I remember they'll chap. "Juliana Josephine Buckingham."

"Pretty. And Buckingham's a nice English name."

I explain again, "My Greek grandfather is so ashamed he doesn't hail from the British Isles that he named himself after the Queen of England's house and married a Scot."

"So your dad is half Greek and half Scot?" X-It says. "Yowie."

"Uh-huh."

"What's your Greek family name then?"

"My grandfather won't tell me. Something–opolis."

"You look more French."

Pleased, I say, "Throw my mother's Anglo-Saxon in there and I'm a classic American mutt."

"A classic American Beauty."

"Cut it out." I want this evening to continue forever.

"If you go see your dad, we can travel partway together."

"I suppose so." The prospect of all that time alone together with X-It makes a trip to see my father very attractive. I shiver. "I guess we should go home soon."

"You sound like you don't want to."

I concentrate on keeping my blades straight. "Why hasn't Penny found a place yet?"

"You still don't like her? She admires you, you know." X-It glances at me. "She just hasn't loved any of places she's looked at."

He shakes out his impact-weary messenger's wrists and I come close to losing my balance.

He continues, "She's so lucky she doesn't have to work. She's free until January when the new semester starts. I wonder what she does all day?"

I keep from falling by leaning forward and grabbing his arm again. "Oh, I'm sure Voodoo keeps her busy chasing her around all day with a hypodermic needle full of some highly addictive substance."

"What?" X-It's face shows pure alarm.

"You haven't noticed Voodoo's turning the gang into addicts one by one? Penny's next."

"No, she's not. I'll have a talk with her. She's thinking of going to Italy over the holidays. I'll make sure she goes."

I'm annoyed at the amount of sway he assumes he holds over Penny's decisions.

Wanting to steer the conversation back to me, I ask, "Do you think I should try to get rid of Voodoo?"

"Why? He's cool." X-It tries a spin on the ice. "He lives a fully realized aesthetic, from his bone structure, to his clothes, to his career."

"Ca-reer?" I squeal as I crash into the wall of the rink. "He deals drugs."

The toddler's mother shoots me another alarmed glance and hustles her child off the ice.

X-It continues as if he didn't hear, "Besides, Penny'd be livid. He's been her friend a long time."

I detect a note of jealousy never present when X-It speaks of Russ.

X-It waits for me to come off the rink's side, and then says, "Voodoo's not as dangerous as he thinks he is."

I just stare at him, and hold out my hand for a final turn around the frozen ring. He grips it and pulls me to him in a dramatic ice-scraping swoosh, then he laughs warmly down into my face. He cannot possibly be gay.

Half frozen, we head to Sixth Street for cheap Indian food rather than face what lies in wait in the refrigerator at home. As a result, we don't reach the apartment until after nine. Mephistopheles and his lotus-eating minions are already out on the town, or rather, the note on my door reads:

> X-It,
>
> Meet us at Dance-o-Matic, Fourth Flr.
>
> Penny

Choosing to ignore the omission of my name and the fact that a note excluding me has been tacked to *my* door, I ask, "Are you going?"

"No. I'm tired. I have to ride in this weather all day tomorrow. Do you need the bathroom? I'm getting in the tub."

"No. You go ahead." I am deflated from head to toe.

I tidy the kitchen then pick up the central room, straightening the floor pillows around the coffee table. My department-store-display palm trees stand nobly in two corners of the room. They date from the Forties. I discovered them in a junk shop. I hung decorative red chili pepper lights from their honest-to-goodness palm fronds. The effect with the pillows enchants me. My apartment was really shaping up before the invasion.

Having my home to myself for a moment is balm on my wounds. However, there remains that funny smell—clove cigarettes mingled with mildewed laundry—which arrived with the unwanted visitors and did not follow them back out the door to Dance-o-Matic.

I pad to the hall and fish my keys from my hanging coat to unlock the dead bolt on my door. I weigh them in my hand. What would happen if I changed the locks on the front door? Can it be done at nine o'clock at night, and accomplished before the revelers stumble home in the early hours?

Oh, what's the use, X-It would just let them in, or give them his key.

I turn the key in the dead bolt to my bedroom. My door swings open. I take three steps into the room and scream.

X-It tears into my room, dripping, wrapping a towel about him. "What the—?"

He stops beside me and stares at the place where my eyes are glued. The candles in each mannequin arm are lit. Dammit, my room was *locked*.

Like a B-movie vampire, Voodoo sits up behind the chaise lounge, laughing.

I stride over to my five-fingered wall sconces and viciously pinch the fire out of each wick.

Voodoo ignores my temper by patting the chaise. "X-It, come here. I want to show you something."

X-It pads over, leaving wet footprints, and peers across the settee. Voodoo produces a black leather box.

"Would you like to see what I keep in here? Some new stuff arrived in the mail today."

I spin around. "Here? In my mail?"

"Where else?" His face is all innocence. "J.J. be a dear and run to the store. The milk went sour. I'll keep X-It company while you're gone."

Oh my god. Voodoo's next target isn't Penny, it's X-It. I have to get him out of here.

"We can't stay," I say. X-It looks at me, curious. "We're leaving now to buy train tickets." I smile at him. "Go get dressed and packed. I'm buying you a ticket!"

X-It shrugs, shakes wetness from his hair, and smiles coyly at Voodoo before leaving the room.

"Nicely played." Voodoo stands up.

I could kill him. He lost the goddamn bet. X-It is *off-limits*. "Get out."

"As you wish."

It occurs to me that perhaps Voodoo considered our agreement to cover only a sexual conquest of X-It, not a seduction into hard drug use. "I'm locking my door when I leave," I say.

His creepshow laugh echoes throughout my apartment.

I stuff most of my clothes into a paper grocery sack, put on my coat, and am ready to go. In the back of my mind is the thought of calling the police while X-It and I are out of town.

"Can we take the bus instead of the train? I'm a little low on funds." I say to X-It as I fold my slim wallet into my coat pocket.

"Yeah. Sure." He pouts. "But train on the way back then."

I'm thrilled he's thinking about us together for the return trip too. I'm more than willing to buy the train tickets. Maybe Mim and Pip, my grandparents, will give me some Christmas money. "Deal," I say.

X-It and I spend the night propped against each other in hard plastic chairs at the bus station. He doesn't mind because the image we make fits some kind of cinematic idea he has in his head. My stiff muscles are penance for something; I don't know what.

We board the bus to Philadelphia in the dark hours of the morning, after a vending machine breakfast of cheese-flavored crackers filled with peanut butter. I settle into the overly tall seat of the touring bus. With my small stature, the seat gives me the impression of an animate throne, peering down to get a good look at me.

When fields have largely replaced suburbs, X-It lays his hand on mine and says in a sleepy drawl, "That was sexy, standing in your room wearing a towel. Do you remember the night you…"

He trails off and I don't have the heart to force his phrase. He might refer to the night I wore only a towel, and I sensed him behind me. His cowardice that night added up to my rejection.

He whispers, "Do you like oral sex?" Sometimes he can be outrageous. Shocking me could be another way of pushing me away.

I have no experience, so I choose silence.

He moves in even closer and says, "When I was a kid I had this babysitter, this guy from next door, who would suck on my penis."

Horrified, I blurt, "Oh, I'm sorry."

"That's okay. I liked it."

I know what happened to X-It is deeply wrong, but I haven't read any of the books and articles that would tell me why. I can't explain it to him. My thoughts fail my emotions. I say, "Oh."

"Has anything like that ever happened to you?" he asks.

Although I never couched it in those terms, as soon as the words were out of his mouth, I knew that it had. Cowed into a confession by the blunt honesty of his own, I say, "When I was ten, almost eleven, my Dad called me into his room on a Sunday morning. When I walked in, I saw right away that his, you know, was outside his underwear. He was grinning at me."

"Oh," says X-It.

I stammer, aghast I've accused a man who now can't defend himself, "I don't think it was really a perv thing. It was more like he was behaving like a little boy and just wanted to see what my reaction would be. He crashed his airplane two months later."

"Is he dead? Oh, wait, he can't be, you're going to see him, right?"

"He's brain damaged. His mother takes care of him."

"Oh." Quite a lot of scenery goes by outside the bus window. Smells of diesel fuel make me think of airplanes.

X-It pushes up the armrest, "Can I lay on you?"

Without hesitation, I extend my hands and gather him into my arms.

CHAPTER NINE

From the Philadelphia bus station, I watch the bus carrying X-It to D.C. as it pulls out onto the road. It belches a farewell cloud of black smoke. If only I could have stayed on the bus with him. With X-It gone, I realize I haven't made any formal arrangements with Mim, my grandmother, which is unfortunate, because Mim is a formal person.

My grandmother's life's work has been to separate herself from her humble Scottish immigrant beginnings through the liberal use of teacups and table linens. I fumble for change then phone my grandparents' house.

They live in the British-sounding suburb of Hatboro, so named because it was initially a millinery town. But I don't have a hat to cover my purple hair, and the time it will take for my grandfather to get to the bus station is just enough time for a dye job.

I enter the bus station bathroom and pull a bottle of China Black hair dye from my grocery sack. Black is the only effective choice if I want to hide all traces of purple. It's a shame to have to cover up my intricate dye job. Oh well, it was half grown out anyway. My hands shake with nerves caused by a public display of hair dying and the impending meeting with my relations.

Two black women come in, avail themselves of the facilities, and wash their hands in the sink furthest away. They shake their heads and leave. They seem so normal and no-nonsense that red shame creeps up my neck. Black dye splashes on the white sink. In the mirror I see it running down my temple. Dammit. That will leave a stain on my skin. I reach for paper toweling from the wall dispenser and a tear-shaped drop lands on my cheekbone below my eye. It looks like a tattoo. I leave it.

I wait for my grandfather. By the time an old blue Chevrolet pulls to the curb, I feel ancient. The driver leans toward me and stares pitifully behind bottle-glass lenses. There is no way Pip, my grandfather, will recognize me, so I open the car door, which releases a blast of lemon air freshener, and climb in.

"Are you a hooker?" He blinks, his eyes magnified three times their normal size. I have the absurd urge to honk his Mr. Magoo nose.

"Pip, it's me, Juliana, your granddaughter."

He threads his fingers, clad in vinyl winter gloves.

"Oh. Good," he says, but appears a bit disappointed. "You don't look the same since I saw you last."

"You haven't changed at all." He wears the same Fifties overcoat and hat I remember as a child.

The drive through the city is largely silent. I catch a glimpse of Independence Hall, and later, the art museum and its many steps sitting above the river. After exiting the Schulkyll Expressway, the Chevrolet winds its way through interminable miles of suburbs. On the sides of the roads, what was snow in New York is slush in Philadelphia. I try to remember why I wanted to come. Did I want to do this? I am counting the days until X-It and I will journey home together. I miss him already.

"Bread," says Pip. "Mim told me to get bread at the store."

His statement doesn't seem to require an response, so I stay quiet.

At the store, Pip mumbles as he shuffles up and down the aisles, "Butter, biscuits, bananas…"

I tug at the sleeve of his overcoat. "Pip, you said Mim asked you to get bread. The bread's over here."

"So it is."

The Chevrolet pulls into the long driveway and rolls across the bucolic bridge over a small stream that graces the front yard. The house is set well back from the road. At the sight of it, my stomach churns, as if attempting to digest carpet tacks. Pip lets himself in the door from the garage without speaking or looking back at me. I guess he means for me to follow him.

Mim stands near the stove; she wears a starched apron over a neat peach-colored polyester pantsuit and stirs a saucepan of what smells like spaghetti sauce with Italian sausage. Mim's lemony scent of Jean Naté body spray mingles with the odors of dinner. Her tower of fiery red hair doesn't move, but her face shakes as she says, "Didn't expect you for the Holidays. But then if you'd bother to write your Dad a letter, you might've told us."

In the early days after my father's accident, about six month's after Mim had stormed our home with a battle cry of he will not go into a nursing home. I was ten. She took custody of my father, fresh out of a coma, away from my shell-shocked mother, and then served her with divorce papers that had Mim's name at the bottom.

I wonder if my mother had officially divorced my father instead of Mim, if she would be dating men with all their parts today?

I'd written my father lots of letters here at the house Mim bought with his money, only to find out that Mim scanned them for any bit of information that could be used against my mother. I stopped writing letters.

"Did you get the pumpernickel and mustard?" Mim says to Pip.

"Wah?" He turns to Mim as he starts to take off his overcoat. He has one shoulder free. "Yes. I got the bread." He sets the loaf on the counter.

"That's not pumpernickel. And where's the mustard? You'll have to go back."

"Oh." He shrugs his overcoat back on and begins a hunt for his car keys.

"They're in your pocket," Mim says. "And hurry back for dinner. I can't get Jack in his chair by myself."

Pip frowns and leaves through the door to the garage.

Mim turns to me, wooden spoon in hand, "Well don't you want to say hello to your father? He's in the living room."

I walk through the dining room with its china cabinet and sideboard, and stick my head around the corner into the living room. My father sits in a recliner. He wears a red plaid chamois shirt and smokes a pipe. A Samoyed dog lays beside him on the carpet. The Eagles game plays on the television. He forms an image of perfect male domestic contentment. I fight a sucking vortex of weird. I've been thrust into a live tableau of what's wrong with this picture?

My father was handsome, but now the back of his skull is oddly flat. The circle of scar tissue mimicks male pattern baldness. The cynical glint that used to sparkle in his pre-accident eyes is replaced with vacant glassiness. His arms and legs, which flew his plane and drove his Lotus, are shriveled and bent, long healed from the multiple operations it took to piece them together. Large metal braces imprison his legs, which stick out into the living room, supported by the recliner's footrest.

"Aaagh! Morugh! Ughh!" Dad flails and thrashes in the chair, his limbs jerk like a B-movie monster's. Did he see me? Is this his reaction? The dog raises its head. I am paralyzed.

Mim rushes in and swipes fallen pipe ash out of the recliner.

"Jack, you know you need to be more careful," she scolds.

Still peering from the doorway, I gape at my grandmother.

"The Good Lord knows he's got few enough pleasures in life," Mim snaps and then glowers. Her cataract-green eyes dare me to utter a syllable. Spine erect and nostrils flared, she returns to the kitchen.

I edge into the living room. "Dad?"

He doesn't hear me. I move closer to the chair. "Dad? It's me, Juliana, I've come to be with you for the Holidays."

He shows no reaction.

I move to stand in front of the recliner and try again, a bit louder, "Hi, Dad. It's Juliana."

"GEROU TH'WAY," He rips off his right leg brace and hurls it at me. I jump back, terrified, once again a two-year-old girl about to pee her pants when faced with her father's anger.

"I-AH," he wheezes. "WAH-CHEN EAGLE'S GA-AME!"

"All right," I say and sit on the edge of a wingback chair.

Mim comes in, sets her mouth at me, heaves a little sigh at my inadequacies, and then leaves the room again. My dad shakily grabs the pouch of tobacco from the lamp stand, somehow manages to pack his pipe, and then reaches for a book of matches.

I massage my eyebrows.

He strikes the match with such trembling force it shoots out into space. The dog yelps and runs to hide behind my chair. I reach my arm back and surreptitiously search its fur.

Mim strides back in and addresses my father, "I told you to be careful. If you'd been more careful to begin with you wouldn't be in that chair!" She removes her apron and balls it up in fury. "How am I supposed to get dinner made?" She lights his pipe and returns once more to the kitchen. The embers in the pipe's bowl glow red as my father inhales.

I depart the wingback chair and inch toward the kitchen, being careful not to block my dad's view of the game. "Is there something I can help you with Mim?" I ask gingerly.

"You came here to visit with your father," Mim says without turning around. "Go visit."

I sidle back to the chair and content myself with scratching behind the dog's ears while I watch the miniature Christmas village under the tree. I think back to the magical moments with X-It in Rockefeller Plaza. Damn Currier and Ives and Bing Crosby anyway. I don't want a White Christmas, I want to white out Christmas. Whatever X-It faces in Virginia, it can't be this bad.

Pip returns with the pumpernickel but no mustard. He's about to turn around and head back to the store when Mim stops him. It's time for dinner. Mim stubs out her cigarette. With their arms beneath Jack's armpits, she and Pip flank him and use the impetus provided by rapidly lowering the recliner's footrest to propel him to his feet.

"Use your knees, Jack. How do you ever expect to walk again if you don't use your knees?"

My grandparents struggle under his weight. I know better than to offer to help. Mim chooses to view me as either a useless child or an unfeeling daughter, whichever suits her purpose at the moment.

My dad's mode of eating makes a mockery of the tablecloth and china, which includes items nonexistent in my childhood experience such as butter dishes, salad plates, and dainty little cream pitchers. He holds his fork in a toddler grip. His torso sways back and forth in an attempt to follow his wavering forkful of spaghetti, which lands more often than not on the tablecloth. If a successful fork to mouth trajectory is accomplished, he opens his mouth with a great snorting inhalation of air before he closes it upon the food.

I pick at my dinner.

"You eat like a bird," comments Mim. "I've kept my figure, you know." My grandmother squints at me. She looks jealous.

"Yes, Dear," says Pip.

Mim answers Pip as if I'm not present. "Young people know all about sex now." She glances at me again. "She probably knows more than I do."

Unable to prevent it, I flash on the French linoleum salesman and Rockabilly Russ. I know I'm turning red.

"See?" says Mim, as if this is proof.

I think of Pyro, Dogbite, and Voodoo back in New York. Their drugged and drooling faces loom up at me from my china. Perhaps I do fall short as a dutiful daughter and granddaughter. A sudden desire to wear a cashmere sweater and pearls and be enrolled at Good Girl U. swamps me.

But it passes. Its lingering effect causes me to say, "I'd like to make some Christmas presents for my aunts, uncles, and cousins. I arrived a bit early, I've got time."

"Yes, you did," says Mim tersely. She pauses for thought. "Your cousin Franz likes fruitcake. No one ever makes it."

"Fruitcakes for all then." I look at Pip. "I'll make a shopping list."

Pip starts to rise. "I'll get my keys."

"Let's go tomorrow, Pip, Okay? I'll go with you."

"You will not," says Mim. "You are here to visit with your father."

I shrug at Pip. Another forkful of spaghetti plops down onto the white linen. I wonder if all this enforced independence isn't more humiliating for my father than a little aid would be.

After dinner, Pip takes off his shirt, clears the table, and washes the dishes. He wears the now wrinkled apron over his sleeveless scooped neck undershirt. His grey, Greek chest hairs poke out. Mim sits at the table with her two constant companions, a cigarette and a cup of Lipton's tea with bitter lemon. She has a large mole on one arching, red-penciled eyebrow. I try not to look at it.

Jack is back in his chair and watching another football game. Is he aware the teams have changed? His dog lies once again by his side. He moves to dump the smoldering pipe ash in the ashtray and manages to get it on the arm of the recliner instead.

Mim jumps up to the rescue. "Jack, be careful."

With my finger I trace the patterns left on the tablecloth by the fallen spaghetti. I will not give Dad a homemade fruitcake for Christmas. I will get him a personal fire extinguisher.

CHAPTER TEN

A current of warm Florida air blows a storm in off the coast and across Philadelphia. Snow turns to sleet, sleet turns to rain, and it rains all night.

In the morning, I wake and peer out the window to a changed landscape. The snow that yesterday decorated the front yard like white cotton batting on a Hollywood Christmas movie set is now pulled back and the ugly brown grass revealed like the floor of a soundstage, a reminder of the reality on which everything rests.

The flooded creek winds through the yard like a swollen, pregnant snake. I rush into my clothes, still pulling on my boots as I clamber from the guest bedroom, across the house, and into the kitchen.

A column of smoke rises from the cigarette in the ashtray next to a cup of tea with lemon. "You'll need to change," says Mim. "We're taking Jack to church this morning."

I pull my arm through the sleeve of my coat and push my way outside. The air feels dangerous. I walk to the bucolic little bridge over the driveway. Water laps around it, a few more inches and it will be flooded over. My hands grip the arching wooden guardrail. The water, the color of coffee *light*, serves as a ferocious antidote to the tiny cups of tea and bitterness inside. *Church?*

My father was an atheist, before the accident. My father had said he didn't much care for his mother, before the accident.

The water moves quickly underneath me and makes me dizzy. The creek's original banks are well underwater. Movement on the edge of the stream near the waterlogged grass catches my attention.

"Oh no!"

A muskrat scrabbles for footing and loses. Its head is just visible in the swirling water.

"Oh, hang on…" But as I say it I know there's nothing I can do. The muskrat's terrified face twirls round and round as the current catches it. In just a few seconds it travels downstream, under the larger bridge of the roadway, and out of sight.

I sink to my knees and cry.

A car pulls in the driveway and honks at me to get off the bridge. I pull myself up and slog to the house, my boots squelching.

"Juliana? Is that you?" A car door shuts and Gloria, the same busybody nurse who found my letter, bustles up behind me. "Look at you, still slim as a reed."

Gloria smells nice, rose water. She resembles a cheery and harmless, pin stripes and lace, Victorian housemaid. But I know better.

"My, don't you look a drowned rat," says Gloria.

Tears threaten. I hold them off.

"You'd better get yourself in a nice warm shower. Here, I brought some of Angie's clothes for you. Mim called and said you don't have anything suitable for church."

I take the bag.

"Best hurry dear. We don't want to be late for services."

Warm water always has an uplifting effect on me. Despite the rain, the muskrat, Dad, Mim, and now Gloria, I sing in the shower. The notes bounce off the walls and caress me with comfort.

My voice rises over the noise of the showerhead singing Ultravox, *"This means nothing to me-e-e. Oohh, Vienna!"*

When I get out, my mood is so improved that I hazard a splash of Mim's Jean Naté . Not bad. Kind of refreshing. I towel dry and puff some powder on my skin. The dress from Gloria's daughter errs on the side of ruffles, and the strappy platform shoes are a tad disco. I style my hair in soft waves away from my face and then assess the total effect in the mirror.

Pretty. Eligible for admission to Good Girl U.

Outside the church, Mim and Gloria speak of me as if I'm not behind them.

"She has a nice voice."

"It needs to be properly channeled."

Mim and Gloria nod at one another and say in unison, "Church choir."

As Mim, Pip, and Gloria struggle to get Jack into his wheelchair, I look up at the tidy red brick church with white trim. Baptist? I puzzle. Mim and Pip aren't Baptists. I stride to where Gloria now pushes Jack along the walkway and Mim and Pip follow.

"Did my dad choose this church?"

Gloria smiles. "This is my church dear. It belongs to all of you Buckinghams now." The nurse turns her attention to maneuvering the wheels toward the front door, wearing the satisfied expression of a hunter with several ducks slung over her shoulder.

I continually adjust my bony seat bones on the wooden pew. The largely incomprehensible sermon of dutiful sin, or sinful duty, washes over me. How easy my life would be if I could just click into place and accept what the pastor is saying as my inner truth. But it isn't, and I can't, so I turn my attention to the choir. Cherry-cheeked blondes in bright blue satin robes sing their hearts out like bluebirds of happiness.

After the service, the reason for Jack's conversion becomes clear, The Chalet Pancake House. Pip is kind enough to tell me that brunch after church is Jack's Sunday tradition. I sit next to my father as he inhales a tall stack.

Gloria and Mim continue their previous discussion about me.

Mim nods sagely and swirls her tea. "She could attend Penn State. Her father—was that a wink?—would pay for that."

"And stay with you folks until she got established," adds Gloria.

Mim says, "And sing in the church choir and come to breakfast with us every Sunday."

Softened by the earlier compliment to my singing, I imagine this scenario. I try to picture my dark and pointed face in a blue robe amongst the cheeky singing cherubs, singing my heart out and winning Mim's approval at last.

A piece of pancake, soft and sticky, flung from my father's fork, hits me in the face. In order not to embarrass Dad, I remove it quickly and act as if it didn't happen. But it's enough to wake my wits.

Mim and Gloria are intentionally not including me in their conversation. They are laying out a scenario and trying to make it as attractive as a decoy duck is to the real thing, and then before I know it, I'll be slung over the hunter's shoulder. But I don't throw out the idea entirely. Attending Good Girl U, with a family to support me, is tempting.

CHAPTER ELEVEN

The next day, I hide in the bathroom in my swimsuit, or more accurately my cousin Hildy's swimsuit borrowed for the occasion. To waste time, I open the cabinet and peruse its contents. Every conceivable Jean Naté product shares the space with boxes of pink Feenamint. All that diuretic tea must require an intestinal antidote. I close the cabinet and look for something else to postpone my father-daughter swim.

Dad swims daily for therapy in the indoor pool, which was added onto the back of the house and paid for out of the settlement from the aviation company. I'm pleased there will always be money for my father's needs, and also perversely pleased that I've been written out of the will, and will therefore be free of whatever karma has attached itself to that money. On the other hand, proof of my father's love is by no means an assured birthright.

A knock sounds.

"Are you done in there?" queries Mim. "I'd like to shave my legs. The attendant has your father in the water already."

I grab a bath towel and crack open the door.

"Come on out with you," Mim urges. "We're going to the shopping mall later this afternoon and my legs need to be beautiful."

Mim stretches a vein-covered ankle through the doorway and waggles her foot. I open the door completely.

"You don't have to worry about the attendant." My grandmother slides against the doorframe, sticks out her bony hip and lowers her crepe eyelids a la Lauren Bacall. "I 'put out the bait' before I hired him. He didn't take it. He's safe."

I struggle to keep my expression blank and pull the small bath towel more tightly around my torso.

The chill of the trip down the hallway is replaced by the humid warmth of the indoor pool room. I enter and close the door in a way I hope won't garner any attention, and then sit on the bench by the wall. Dad bobs in the water near the side of the pool, which has been specially equipped with bars for the handicapped. The attendant is nowhere in sight. I sit, beads of moisture accumulating on my face, and watch the bald flat spot on the back of my father's head dip up and down.

"It's okay to get in." The attendant's voice behind me causes me to jump and the towel falls to the bench. I turn to look at him and am surprised to find a gentle-faced, middle-aged man, apparently none the worse for having survived Mim's putting out of the bait.

"Don't you need to watch him?" I ask.

"I'm never far. This is the time of day your grandmother does her toiletries. Your dad likes a moment alone. He knows what to do as far as his exercises go." The attendant winks.

I won't argue with that, and decide to go ahead and swim. The bathwater-warm liquid envelopes me in its chlorinated embrace. I swim a couple of lazy laps and then rest in a corner, my arms on the sides. The motion of my swimming alerts Jack to my presence and he slowly rotates to stare at me. I try a shy smile and hope he doesn't wear his leg braces in the pool.

He's looking at me, no, leering at me, in a way that no father should ever look at his daughter. Unnerved, I use my hands to crawl along the pool's edge to the stepladder. As I hoist myself out of the water, my wet hands slide on the wide metal railings. His intense lecherous gaze travels up my dripping legs to my swimsuit. He doesn't recognize me as his daughter.

The same crawling disbelief and betrayal I experienced when I was ten years old rises from my belly. But when he called me into his room and exposed himself all those years ago, he knew who I was, and surely must have been teasing.

My feet slip on the tile.

Grateful the attendant is turned away as he stacks towels, I sprint for the safety of the hallway. Hildy's suit is heavy and dripping. It's cold outside the pool room, but I can't retreat to the main bathroom because Mim is defoliating.

I dry my quivering legs with the chenille bedspread in the guest bedroom. I throw on a vintage men's gabardine shirt, buttoned up to my neck, some funky wool pants that really require suspenders, slick back my black hair, and travel to the kitchen where I corner Pip.

"Get your keys," I say to his surprised magnified eyes. "We're getting some cherries and citron. We'll bring that home, and then head back to the store for the nuts and rum."

* * *

The fruitcakes are out of the oven and line the countertop like small sarcophagi. Their aroma intoxicates me, and I assert silently that they are a most unfairly maligned holiday treat.

Mim gives my father his daily typing lesson in the other room. Sounds of tapping and labored breathing, which accompany his concentrated efforts, float into the kitchen and mingle with the soundtrack to Wonder Woman from the living room. Pip does enjoy watching Lynda Carter.

I uncap the rum.

Mim's voice wins out over the sound of bullets being reflected off of golden bracelets. "The word is 'time,' Jack, not 'term.' 'Now is the time for all good men to come to the aid of their country.' You've done this a hundred times."

I splash all of the golden loaves with the rum.

Mim continues, "Jack, it's 'good men' not 'hood men.'" She sniffs.

"I smell alcohol. You were drinking the night you got in that plane, weren't you? Your sisters and I knew you'd taken to drink. It was that Carla, and working for her father, wasn't it?"

Carla is my mother. I empty the rum bottle onto the now soaking little cakes.

"Focus on each key. Use the tip of each finger. You thought you were so high and mighty running that company for him. You treated me like a poor relation when I came to visit. A poor relation. Sit up straight."

I get out the plastic wrap and shroud each potent fruitcake. I stack them like bricks at the back of the counter, where they will mellow until Christmas. There are no sounds coming from the other room. I wash my hands and go see. Mim has removed the typewriter from in front of my father and replaced it with a checkbook. She holds his hand and is "ghost-writing" his signature on the checks. She stands up stiffly when she sees me.

"He's competent." She glowers. "The judge said so. Get ready to go to the mall. You need to be out of here by two-thirty."

Mim's lawyer, Mr. Strutherford, advised her to have Jack declared competent, with her having power of attorney. That way their affairs and books cannot be looked into by any other party, concerned or not.

Mim clicks into the kitchen; her camel-colored Naturalizer shoes match her winter coat; their buckles match her earrings.

She adjusts the silk scarf around her neck and says, "Your aunt's in the driveway. We need to go." She just has time to drain her teacup and stub out her cigarette before ushering me out the door.

What is the rush? Braving the disapproving scrutiny of my aunt, I pull together my thrift store coat and get in the car. Another vehicle turns in the driveway, bumps over the bridge and parks as we're leaving. Mim and my aunt exchange a meaningful glance.

At the mall, Mim purchases Love's Baby Soft products and Polo blouses for my cousins, Hildy and Marie. My aunt drowned her half-Greek heritage by marrying a man of non-dilute German ancestry, and naming her ensuing blond children Franz, Hildegard, Kurt, and Marie.

A stray punk girl with raccoon eyes and straggly pink hair stares at me as I pass. My current outfit is not an effective disguise. I could douse myself in Love's Baby Soft and wrap myself in Polo blouses to no effect. I admit, the hair dye teardrop tattoo doesn't help matters.

Riding the escalators is the most fun generated in the mall this afternoon, which isn't much. I glance down at the glittering department store, decked in holiday cheer, as it spreads out beneath me with every ascending stair of the escalator. Suddenly overheated in my old lady coat, I fight the urge to barf on all the glossy shoppers below, who I'm sure dislike me on sight as much as Mim and my aunt do.

The department store would make a fantastic nightclub. This thought sticks X-It into the forefront of my mind with the accuracy of a switchblade. I ache to be able to laugh with him. I want to slide my arms around his waist, hold on to his firmness. I long to kiss him.

I should have stayed on the bus.

My thoughts are rattled by snippets of conversation from Mim and my aunt, riding a few steps behind.

"Thank God we got her out of the house in time."

"…imagine getting paid for that…"

"…filthy, but necessary…"

"…she's a doctor…"

"He get's so worked up on the days she comes…"

I put two and two together; I was ushered out of the house to avoid seeing my father's sex therapist. I add this information to my morning's nightmare in the pool, and come close, not to vomiting, but to passing out. My army boots meet the unmoving edge of the department store floor as the escalator ends.

I stumble forward and fall into a clutch of mannequins dressed for a New Year's Eve party. Smiling down on me like angels of salvation are Karisma, Carol Alt, and Joan Severance. Their eyes twinkle at me and I know I stare up into the faces of my own labor. Somewhat restored, I right myself by pulling up on Karisma's shoulders. I kiss the mannequin's cheek, to the consternation of a salesclerk and the mortification of my relatives.

That evening, I can't bring myself to look Mim or my father in the face and converse mostly with Pip.

He turns to Mim and mentions casually, "Juliana's grown into a fine looking young woman, don't you agree?"

"She looks like Carla," Mim spits my mother's name.

After dinner—if it's Friday, it must be flying crab cakes—I commit treason. While Mim enjoys her tea and cigarette in the dining room, I sneak into the kitchen and phone my mother. Long distance.

The number is on her latest postcard.

"Hi Mom," I whisper, "I'm at Dad's, with Mim and Pip."

"Oh Honey, why?" The line crackles, as if adding its opinion.

"It's Christmas. I made fruitcakes for everyone."

"They should love you."

"Mom, Mim told Dad he crashed because he was drinking, and he was drinking because he was married to you and worked for Grampa. Is that true?"

"Truth is relative."

"How come Grampa turned his back on us too?"

"He thought divorcing your dad was the wrong thing to do."

Cigarette smoke and lemony Jean Naté hovers near my shoulder.

"Who are you talking to?" asks Mim.

"A friend," say I and hand Mim the receiver. "Here, say 'Merry Christmas.'"

After a few moments of listening to the voice on the other end of the line, Mim goes rigid. The ends of her lacquered mound of red hair come loose and lick toward the ceiling like flames.

"Deserve?" she shouts into the mouthpiece. "You deserve nothing. You abandoned your husband in his time of need. You haven't been here in the trenches. You don't deserve to know how he is."

A cold calm, somewhat close to paralysis, or rigormortis, creeps over me. I back out of the kitchen and continue to back through the dining room into the living room, where I peck my dad with a little goodnight kiss on the top of his head.

"Aaarugh!" He screams as if in pain. His dog quizzes its head. I back away, tears forming. Why do I keep trying?

Pip shuffles in and explains Jack cut his head getting in the car last week and still has a small set of stitches. Expressionless, I back out of the living room and down the hall to the guest room where I shut the door and lock it.

Around midnight, I creep from my room fully dressed, brown paper bag of clothes in hand. In the kitchen I gather all of the fruitcakes into the bag and grab a bottle of rum. With one last look at the darkened Christmas tree and lifeless miniature village in the living room, I say a silent goodbye, grab a pack of Mim's matches off the table, and haul the fruitcakes out to the bucolic bridge over the stream. There, I kneel on the icy tarmac, unwrap each loaf and build a fruitcake pyramid.

The screw cap bounces into the water. Like any pirate worth her mettle, I upend the bottle and glug. Coughing, I pour the rest of the alcohol on the cakes. Sulfur bites my nostrils as I toss a lit match onto the pile and back down the driveway. Flames lick the heavens.

"Glor-or-or-or-or-ria," I sing in a whisper to the wind spirits who encourage the fire.

The only thing left to do is what I do best. I roll up the top of the bag, clutch it to my chest, and take off running.

CHAPTER TWELVE

Outside the Philadelphia bus station in the middle of the night, I feel around in the bottom of the grocery sack for loose change. My victory adrenaline from the fruitcake bonfire has ebbed and is replaced with my familiar fuzzy-felt numbskin of survival mode.

My fingers touch the cold and reaffirming shapes of coins. I need to call someone. X-It? God, I miss him with a physical pain, but I have his parent's address and not the telephone number. My mother? Look what that led to. Michael?

Michael.

I wipe wetness from my eyes with the back of my left hand and awkwardly slam quarters into the pay phone slot with the force of a toddler figuring out a shape-sorter.

Michael told me I could call him anytime, but still I feel embarrassed. When the call picks up, I again ask for Art.

"He's asleep. Is this J.J.?"

"Yes." I choke back a snorting sob.

"Are you okay?" Michael's voice springs to alertness.

"No… " I swallow and stall. Fruitcakes, pipes, scarred scalps, leg braces, teacups and cigarettes flood my thoughts. I push them back under my numbskin and say instead, "He's evil."

"Who?"

"Voodoo. He wants to take X-It away from me."

"X-It doesn't belong to anyone."

Michael's ability to be practical after being woken in the middle of the night is just the tonic I need. My breath slows.

"Voodoo," Michael pauses. "The drug dealer?"

"He's evil." My breath quickens again, and everything hiding under the numbskin attaches itself with full force to the situation I ran away from in New York. "We can't go back."

Michael sighs. "He wishes he was. Look." He yawns. "J.J. I want to help you, but I have to work tomorrow and need to go back to sleep." He yawns again.

"Oh." I can smell my stale breath on the mouthpiece. "Well, thanks. Goodnight Michael."

"Wait a minute, J.J."

"I thought you were tired."

He issues a slightly sexy sounding, "Hmm." His sheets rustle. "What are you wearing?"

"This coat that used to belong to some old dead lady. It's cold outside the bus station."

His voice switches from sensual to shocked. "You're outside a bus station? If it's eleven-thirty here, it's got to be two-thirty there."

"Yeah, I guess so."

"J.J., you really need somebody to take care of you." His sheets rustle again.

It would be warm and cozy next to Michael in his sheets. The edges of my survival numbskin begin to fray. Tears threaten.

"Goodnight Michael," I say hastily.

"Yup, take care of yourself, J.J."

I hang up.

Suddenly, oppressively alone, I sink to the ground and curl my knees to my chin to shut out the night and the cold. I wrap my coat about me. The perfume from the coat's previous owner clings to the threads. Do I wear a dead woman's coat? Was it pried from her lifeless form along with a handbag clutched in stiff fingers? Was this woman loved? Was she missed?

If I freeze in the night outside the bus station, who will remove the coat from my body, forever cast in fetal position? Who will pull the grocery bag from my curled fingers?

Am I loved? Will I be missed?

Who will miss Mim when her final cigarette is stubbed out? I've tried all my life to show Mim I love her, tried to be a good granddaughter. But I now realize as I sit alone on the concrete outside the bus station, Mim doesn't want love; she wants allegiance. And she certainly does not want any competition for her son from a source as legitimate as his daughter.

Dad's lecherous face rises up at me. Weary, I lean my head back against the unmoving strength of the brick wall. Bolstered by Michael's matter-of-fact reassurance and his frank interest in me, I'm slightly ashamed at having run away from New York in hysterics. Voodoo is just a pumped up misfit like the rest of them.

* * *

I bump along, watching the countryside from the windows of a county bus. This bus is sixth in a line of buses I've taken from the D.C. Greyhound station, each successive bus declining in repair and respectability. I've rumbled past symmetrical suburban developments, past columned houses and white-fenced fields of pampered, blanketed horses, and now into a wilderness of chicken wire, squat sagging dwellings, and rotted-out automobiles.

In the tiny town of Higgins, Virginia, the bus stops, heaves, and passes exhaust with the relish of a plow horse in front of a bran mash at day's end. The door folds open and I step into the world of X-It's boyhood. I hope to find the hamlet quaint, but am instantly oppressed by cold, damp poverty.

I ask directions at a gas station convenience store as I pay for my lunch of cheese puffs and a cola. Licking the orange powder from my fingers, I make my way six blocks east and two blocks south. I pass a fence made of iron gates lashed together, tall and rusty, the kind seen around historic cemeteries. Untidy vines, bare now in winter, and evergreen bushes struggle to grow over and around the barrier.

At least thirty old refrigerators are penned inside this gothic zoo. How odd. Odd interests me.

I continue down the broken, askew slabs of sidewalk and step around a child in a snowsuit and mittens who plays with plastic dinosaurs. He must be imagining the jutted slabs are the work of primeval plate tectonics, or at least a volcano.

What is X-It doing right now? And where is his house? The numbers on the mailboxes are too high. I must've passed it. I double back.

According to the house numbers on either side of the peculiar cemetery fence, this is it. I try to force apart a section of iron gate.

"Uh-uh," says the little boy, looking up from his dinosaurs. "That's not the way you go in. Over there." He points to a dirt footpath down the side of the fence.

"Thanks." I return his shy smile with my own.

I start along the path. X-It must have seen me from wherever the house is, because he tears down the path like a guard dog, but instead of tearing me to bits, he clasps my shoulders and shakes me.

"You came. You came for me." His smile spreads all over him.

"Well, not really."

"Sure you did. You're here. Come meet my mom."

I follow him around the back of the refrigerators to a tiny house, as well kept as the yard and fence are unkempt.

"Careful, don't let out the cats," X-It says as I close the door behind me.

X-It motions for me to sit on a worn gold velvet brocade sofa. Something about the cramped rooms and precisely arranged furniture makes me nervous, and I sit on the edge. Sweat prickles my neck and I loosen my coat, but feel more protected leaving it on.

X-It notices I'm over warm as he sits next to me on the arm of the sofa. "Mom's got the heat cranked up. It's bath day." He rolls his shoulders. "Every Tuesday."

He kicks the couch rhythmically with his heel. A huge pair of eyes in a wet face peers around the corner and beams up at me. The small, drenched animal shakes its paws in loathing and shoots across the living room.

A stout woman enters, red-faced, tucking damp strands of hair behind her ears. "Come back here." She bends under the dinette. "You are not dry."

The demon lashes a soggy tail against the woman's arm and growls.

"Mom, I want you to—"

The longhaired cat is carried to the back of the house. A door closes and the sounds of a blow dryer are heard. It's then that I notice five more Persian cats, some licking themselves industriously, others still awaiting their baths, sit around the room on and under furniture.

"They're all purebreds," says X-It.

"Oh."

"With papers."

"Can we go outside?" I run my fingers under my collar.

"Sure, I'll show you our Refrigerator Garden."

Facing the yard from the house is a different visual experience than from the street. Some of the refrigerators have been there a long time and have sunk into the mud.

X-It gestures toward the large white shapes, some rounded, some square. "My dad tried refurbishing appliances for awhile. It didn't pan out."

"Were these here when you were little?"

"Some of them.

"Jeezus, your mother must have been sick with worry. Kids suffocate in these things all the time. You should tell that neighbor boy to stay out of here."

X-it rolls his shoulders and I thread my way around iceboxes that look like giant's teeth stuck in the ground. The tooth fairy would be bankrupt in a day. I laugh.

"What's funny? I know it's a bit unusual, but isn't it cool?"

"Sure. I think I'm just a bit lightheaded. I need to eat." I gesture at the refrigerators. "You should draw them."

X-It jumps and looks frightened. "Draw? Not here. Come on, I'll find you some food."

I sit at the dinette as X-It rustles in the kitchen, and a moist Persian cat rubs against my leg. The only sign of Christmas is a small artificial tree on a shelf in the corner, well up and away from the cats. There are no framed pictures from X-It's childhood. Instead, Persian pedigrees line the wall. I'm disappointed. I want to know what he looked like when he was little.

X-It places a plate of cold ham and fixings in front of me. Saliva floods my mouth. The cheese puffs are all I've had to eat since leaving Mim's. I eat greedily and a cat meows from beneath the table.

The front door opens and in walks a man in a dark blue jumpsuit, zippered up the front. He smells of diesel fuel.

"Hi Dad, I'd like you to meet—"

"God Damn it, is that the ham?" The man grows larger and seems to almost touch the ceiling of the small house. I shrink in my chair.

"Dad, this is my friend from New York."

"Another stray. What did we tell you about bringing home any more strays! Dammit that ham was dinner." He is truly furious.

The ham sticks in my throat. My eyes water and I fear I'll cough the bite of food onto the table.

His dad walks up to me, taking in my hair and clothing.

"New York, huh?" He turns to X-It. "When are you gonna stay down here and get yourself a real job. There's money drivin' truck. Pansy-assed bicycles. Shit."

X-It's mother appears, holding a fluffy Persian in one arm and a brush in her other hand.

"What are you getting so worked up about, Percy?" Percy points to me. My fork is frozen in mid-air.

"Sweet Charity." His mother sets down the brush. "Oh, but this does push the limits."

I swallow and speak, "X-It, I think I'd better go."

"His name's Thomas!" his mother shrieks.

"For all the good it does him," says his father. "Elgine, I told you adopting a baby is like getting a dog from the pound. But you had to have one. Look at those lips, he's got darkie blood. It's obvious, but you won't see it."

I look at X-It's beautiful features, pale eyes and white blond hair. Have they washed all the color out of him? I spring to my feet. "X-It, come with me."

"Thomas," orders his mother. "You will stay here."

X-It runs to get his things.

"Aw, let him take his darkie, art-fag ass back to New fucking York." His dad sits down and begins to eat my ham.

X-It pushes me out the door ahead of him. He turns, and right before he slams it, screams back, "Yeah, well at least I've got papers!"

CHAPTER THIRTEEN

I pay for Amtrak tickets home. Home is New York. Home is our apartment. Home is doing our laundry and going to the corner grocery together. We'll be home for Christmas.

A nor'easter blows across the eastern seaboard. The train makes its way in the darkness between stations, with ever increasing amounts of white flurries showing under the platform lights at each stop northward. X-It and I were lucky to get seats. The cars are full of holiday travelers. My grocery sack suitcase is crammed overhead amongst the countless square shapes of more legitimate luggage. I ball up my coat for a pillow and press it between my cheek and the frosty glass of the window.

X-It's head lies in my lap, as serene as a toddler in sleep. I marvel at the brilliance inside his heavy cranium, his rapid-fire creativity and exacting hand-eye coordination.

Why did X-It go home for Christmas? I don't know. All I know is that Percy and Elgine and Mim and Pip and even Jack are eating and breathing and moving through this world. There must be some pay-off that keeps them shoveling food in their mouths everyday.

Mim's pay-off is manipulation. Pip's is a jelly donut. Elgine is easy: purebred Persians. Percy? I figure that as long as there's someone below him in the social hierarchy, he'll get up everyday and put on his blue, zippered jumpsuit.

What about Jack, my father? What can a soul learn from an awareness so diminished? I don't know. But I know it's not Mim's voice he gets up for every day. Maybe he gets up because his heart is still beating, and his ability to question why his heart is still beating just isn't there.

What about me? What's my payoff?

It's in my lap.

I smile down at X-It. As long as I have him to love, to urge on to greatness, I will keep painting mannequins and paying the rent.

* * *

The key turns in the lock and the door to my apartment swings open. I breathe a sigh of relief. The dwarves appear to be out. The place is a mess. As promised by Voodoo's good-bye laugh, the heavy door to my bedroom is slightly ajar. I push it open, expecting to find my belongings ransacked and signs of takeover habitation. But everything is strangely as I left it.   Although from the scent of Voodoo's hair product I detect, he may have slept in here.

The first thing X-It does is turn on his radio and make sure it still works. I hear him jumping from station to station in the other room.

After tossing my grocery sack in the corner, I grab a rag and some cleanser. I scour and tidy the rest of the apartment. Somehow, ridding my dwelling of take-out cartons and dirty glasses with cigarette butts floating in them helps rid me of that awful dangling feeling left by going to see my father. X-It turns up Stiff Little Fingers and I find myself whistling

I move a pillow. Beneath it lies a hypodermic needle, small and slender with an orange plastic plunger. Traces of blood and clear fluid remain in the very tip. Part of me is intrigued, and that part allows me to hold the syringe up to the light, to turn it this way and that, and to see a small drop of fluid gather seductively at the needle's sharp tip.

I chuck it in the trashcan under the kitchen sink.

86

X-It breezes in. "It looks pretty good in here now," he says. "Do you wanna go get something to eat?"

A door in the back of the apartment creaks open slowly. Is Voodoo here after all?

"G'dye," says Crikey. Dressed only in boxers, he rubs his stubble-covered face. "I've got a bloomin' headache."

"Oh Christ, it's you," I say.

He stumbles past us into the kitchen and fetches a glass of water.

"Well it's nice to see you too, J.J. We thought you'd scarpered off." He takes a long drink. "It all seems a bit pointless without you."

"What do you mean?" I stay behind X-It, taking comfort in his proximity.

"Voodoo's restless like, doesn't have a direction, no purpose. He was that way in San Francisco too, after you left."

I squeeze X-It's arm.

"Don't you think that's a bit weird?" I ask Crikey.

"Maybe he's in love with ya."

I snort. X-It gives my hand an answering squeeze.

Water glass in hand, Crikey turns around to face us with a quizzical look on his face. I issue a tiny gasp.

"What?" Crikey sucks his chin into his neck in puzzlement.

"Your chest. Look at it."

We file to the bathroom. Crikey explores the blood-beaded scratches on his pecs.

"Strewth, I don't remember those." Crikey makes a face as he leans closer to the mirror.

X-It runs his fingers along the cuts.

This sudden act of intimacy makes me feel like an intruder.

"Salt on your fingers stings a bit," says Crikey.

X-It asks, "Do you want me to stop?"

"No."

"You better wash those out," I say. "They're not deep enough to scar but they could get infected."

"Thanks, Mum," says Crikey.

X-It laughs, and I want to hit him.

"X-It," I say, knowing he can't resist. "Let's sketch together."

X-It and I stay in my room, drawing with the door shut until well into the evening. He sketches fantasy models wearing his clothing designs and I draw the Refrigerator Garden from memory. The front door opens and closes several times, but each time X-It rises to see who it is, I convince him to stay and draw with me.

We get hungry and decide to go and try a cheap new Japanese restaurant on St. Marks Place. Tentatively, I turn the deadbolt knob and look into the entryway. All's clear. I edge out of my room.

A warm mouth clamps on mine and arms encircle me. Patchouli, or some similar awful smell, surrounds me. I struggle to pull away.

The mouth eases off and says, "Look up J.J."

Hung from the entryway ceiling is a bunch of mistletoe.

"Voodoo—really."

I push his arms away and turn to see X-It in my doorway. For the first time ever, he looks jealous. I smile inwardly. For once Voodoo has caused something good to happen.

"Aren't you going to wish me Merry Christmas?" Voodoo asks.

"Aren't you pagan?" I say, brushing off my sweater.

"True, true. But like all fun Christmas traditions, the mistletoe used to be a pagan one. And tonight's the winter solstice. Longest, darkest night of the year and I am going to par-tay. You two coming?"

X-It sidles around me. I will him to grab me, as I'm beneath the mistletoe, and give me the kiss I crave. But he goes toward his room.

"Nah," he answers Voodoo. "Don't feel like it. I'm working tomorrow." He turns. "Still having dinner with me, J.J.?"

"Yes, of course."

Voodoo remains standing too close, invading my personal space.

He grabs my finger with his hand and brings it to his lips. "Are you sure you won't come out, cut up the dance floor, and burn up the town with me tonight in place of a Yule log?"

X-It reappears at my side, wearing his coat. He grabs my hand away from Voodoo. "Come on J.J. Let's eat."

I am struck fresh by my dilemma. How am I going to get Voodoo out of my apartment?

* * *

On Christmas day I receive two presents. The first is that ever since our ill-fated trip to see our parents, X-It clings to me like a lost child. Even Penny can't pull him away. I've never been happier. The second present is a phone call from Michael.

"Merry Christmas!" The joy in his voice is infectious.

I grin, even though I have no tree, tinsel, or festivities to attend.

"What'd you do today?" he asks.

"Not much. X-It and I went out last night and stayed out late."

"I'm at my mom and dad's house. My brother's here and my sister and her husband and kids. It's a crowd." I experience a sudden wrench of homesickness for my mother. I haven't received a new postcard.

I hear laughing children and clinking glasses in the background. Michael's house sounds so normal, so nice, like what I wanted when I thought of Mim's Christmas village while skating in Rockefeller Plaza.

"That's lovely."

"Do you still have your unwanted roommate problem?"

Itchy shame creeps up my neck. I never should have told him. "Uh-huh."

"J.J. I know it's Christmas." Michael clears his throat. "But I think I need to say something to you."

Uh-oh.

"Remember when I called you a 'diamond in the rough'? Well," he takes a breath. "Uncut gems don't get polished by hanging out in the dirt. You need to dump these creepy losers and get to school."

Stung, I feel like he called me a loser.

"Promise me, okay?" he asks.

"What?"

"Promise me you'll go check out art school."

I shrug my shoulders like X-It. "Sure."

We disconnect and Christmas feels a continent away.

CHAPTER FOURTEEN

February, 1981

Perching on my stool in the mannequin factory, I switch paintbrushes to the one with the finest tip, swirl it in China Black, and steady my hand to paint the fluid line that will become eyeliner on the bald head I work on.

The freight elevator at the far end of the factory grinds to a stop and out steps Bela, the eastern European sculptor responsible for Karisma and the others. He rarely descends from his studio. My supervisor and the other five-dollars-an-hour elves sit erect as he comes our way.

Bela holds a flesh-colored fiberglass hand, which he waggles in the supervisor's face. "I need new hands. These are outdated. Find me a hand model."

My supervisor's mouth becomes a thin line. We're already behind on an order. I continue to paint. The others have stopped. Bela observes me closely then says something inaudible to the supervisor.

"Miss Buckingham," says the supervisor, adjusting her glasses. "Hold up your hand."

"Huh?" I look up and narrow my eyes.

"Put down your paintbrush and hold up your hand."

I comply, nonchalantly turning my hand this way and that in the air. Bela comes near, plucks my hand from the air, and holds it close.

"Lovely," he says. "How would you like to make five hundred dollars?"

My interest increases. "Yeah."

Bela drops my hand and converses again with my supervisor. I can only make out part of what they're saying.

"…yes, she is."

"She does not know it…"

"…it's so refreshing when they don't know it."

"…back to work…"

Bela turns and speaks to me, "You will follow me upstairs."

I experience a moment's hesitation. But surely nothing too horrible will be demanded of me. The sculptor motions for me then turns and strides to the elevator. I hurry to follow him.

"Clean your brushes first, Miss Buckingham," the supervisor's voice stops me.

I return to hastily swish my brushes around in turpentine then bolt for the elevator.

Upstairs, Bela's studio is filled with natural light, pieces of mannequins, original body part sculptures, and yellowed company paperwork. All of this detritus has been pushed around the edges of the room. In the center is a stool, and some ways apart, a table with tools.

Bela has me sign some paperwork then instructs me on the differing hand positions he desires. When I have it down, he coats my hands with goo. He gets out two trough-like molds and tells me to position my hands inside them. Plaster is poured, only filling the molds halfway.

As the plaster sets it becomes uncomfortably warm on my skin.

"I thought you sculpted the hands?" I inquire. Bela is very quiet as he works and my words seem an intrusion.

"I do," he finally answers. "I work from the casts so you do not have to sit here for hours. They become my model. Sometimes the hands are so perfect I use the casts and simply smooth them down. Your hands might be such hands. You have hands of an artist, sensitive, but you are not an artist, no?"

"I want to be."

"Is mannequin painter the kind of artist you want to be?" The skin around his eyes crinkles.

My face grows as warm as my hands. "Is mannequin sculptor the kind of artist you wanted to be?"

"No." He looks at me directly from under a white eyebrow. "This is why I ask you. Because you are young and do not have to end up old and lonely, making sculptures no one notices."

"I notice them. I go out of my way to walk past the windows of Saks or Bloomingdale's. I can tell which ones I've painted. They smile at me." I shrink when I realize how crazy that sounds.

The corner of Bela's mouth rises in a wry smile. "Thank you for noticing them. But think of how you would feel to walk in gallery and see your own work on the walls."

He strides to me and lifts my chin. I feel strangely vulnerable, handcuffed, with my hands in the plaster.

He runs his thumb along my jaw line. "In Europe you would be celebrated beauty."

I tilt away, uncomfortable. Then I realize his comment is aesthetic and not sexual. "Why there and not here?"

He says, "Here everything needs to be same. If I make head of you and you see it in Saks window, it stands out. People look at the head and not at the clothes. No good."

"What about Karisma? She's a 'celebrated beauty.'"

"Her features are regular." Bela winks. "Nothing stands out."

"I'd still like to meet her."

"Meet her or be her?" He sighs. "What we need are some good new male mannequins. The ones we have look like eunuchs."

I giggle. "Do they have to be famous models? Or could it be someone I know?"

"You know handsome man?"

I smile as I think of X-It.

"Ah-ha-ha, I see you do!" Bela teases.

But X-It is not typical either, I was referring to Crikey. Maybe this could be a way to get at least him away from Voodoo. "Yes, I know a very handsome man. From Australia."

"Have him call me."

* * *

Taking Bela's words on being an artist to heart, I honor my promise to Michael and call in sick the next day. I will tag along with Penny and check out Parsons. I already increased my salary for the week by hand modeling, so I'm not worried.

Sick with nerves to be going anywhere near an art school, I can't decide what to wear, and settle for my least attention-attracting clothes. What am I doing? They'll all know I'm not an artist. They'll think I look like a poser, as phony as my British-sounding surname. Penny will probably set me up to look bad.

How can I ever attend art school? I don't have a portfolio, don't have any money. Just a lousy GED.

I rub my eyes forgetting I already put on black eyeliner. Shit. Pretty Penny steps over the bodies of the sleeping dwarves in the living room.

"Is X-It gone already?" she asks.

I smile, remembering the peck on the cheek he gave me before taking off. He's happy I'm going to Parsons with Penny. Uh-oh, I sniff and grab for a Kleenex. Goddammit, I'm getting a cold. My nose will run all through Penny's class and I'll have to sit in the corner and pretend I'm not the one making the icky snuffling noises.

I blow my nose. "X-It leaves for work before six every morning. I thought you knew that."

"I'm asleep at six every morning, silly. I'm glad you're coming today." She lifts her portfolio. "Today's critique day and I'm bringing something that will knock this teacher on his ass."

We bustle out the door.

"Is it that good?" I ask.

Her white teeth blind me. "Sure it's good."

Deflated, I can think of nothing to say.

"But this is pure revenge." Penny skips for a few paces. "This teacher thinks he's so cool. He likes to push the limits, ya know?"

"Hmm," I say in what I hope passes for a knowing tone.

"Our current assignment is about portraying sex. I guess Mr. Barrett's bored with the usual stuff. Last week he had the poor model pose with a plaster head in her crotch. And she did it! Because people who get paid ten dollars an hour have no spine—and we had to draw it. Yuck."

I make half that amount of money, so I figure I must have no spine and no legs to stand on either. I trot to keep up with Penny's long strides as we turn onto St. Mark's Place. How much more intimidating can art school get?

Penny says with sophistication, "So just wait 'til you see what subject I picked to do my piece on. It'll make every male in the room squirm."

Oh great. "I'm gonna need coffee for this," I say and duck into an espresso bar.

At Parsons, we climb the stairs to Penny's class. I can't shake the feeling that I do not belong here, that the building will sense my presence and strain me out like a bit of lumpy gesso. In the classroom, I sit at the back in the corner, as I planned, and watch the students pin up their work to be critiqued. I set my tall café latté on the floor next to my chair and hope I don't kick it over.

Oh my god.

Penny steps away from her piece pinned to the wall. All pink, red, and pearlescent, it is an X-rated valentine of a man and woman engaged in anal sex. Penny added glitter.

I've heard people do this, but thought it was pretty much a gay thing. I freely admit I'm a sexual retard. I stare, along with the rest of the class in fascination, and then again along with the rest of the class, look away.

A man in his fifties, wearing a long scarf and wire-rimmed eyeglasses, strides into the room.

"Mr. Bartlett?" Penny catches the instructor's attention. "My friend here is auditing your class today, as a potential student."

Me? My gut floods with acid. The latté was a stupid idea.

Mr. Bartlett gives a brief nod in my direction and turns to observe the assigned work. I sense the students holding their collective breath. But the teacher simply unwinds his scarf and begins to discuss the first piece of art on the far left side of the wall.

The students' images range from insipid kisses and abstract twining bodies, to one scientific rendering of an encounter between sperm and ovum. I have to give Penny credit. She didn't wimp out on the assignment.

The instructor stops in front of a drawing of a woman obviously done by a young male because her breasts are all out of proportion and attach to her torso in an unnatural way. This guy is no X-It.

"Can anyone here tell me how to improve these eyes?" The instructor turns to the room. "They lack focus."

Her eyes? My hand shoots up. I stare up at its betrayal. Mine is the only hand in the air.

"Good, our guest. Go ahead."

"I-I'd rather show you."

"Alright."

I rise and head for the chalkboard, wiping my sweaty palms on my skinny plaid pants. I grab a piece of chalk. It squeaks and breaks on contact. I wipe my palms again and take another breath. Starting over, I outline an almond-shaped eye on the board.

"Okay," I say. "The eyes in this drawing are a bit too close, ideally there is the width of an eye between the two eyes. And this woman's eyes are too high up in her face.

"About the eye itself," I say and draw. My hand takes over and my mouth follows. "The bottom of the iris touches the bottom lid, but the upper lid cuts it off and also casts a shadow." I draw it in. "There is a darker circle around the edge of the iris and the darkest points are the pupils. These need to be placed carefully because they provide the focus, and they often blend into the shadow caused by the upper lid. There is a highlight caused by reflected light here." I dot it. "But the lense is a clear convex shape, so light passes through and this side of the iris is consequently lighter." I rub chalk to indicate the lighter portion then stop and look around. "There are a few other details like the little pink bit at the corner, but that's mostly it."

Everybody claps.

Somebody says, "Are you a grad student?"

"No. I paint mannequins." My nose is about to drip. I sniff. "For a living."

"Very good, thank you," says Mr. Barrett.

I sit down as my legs give way and the instructor moves on to the next piece. I sneak a glance at Penny, whose lower lip is out at being upstaged.

Sensing my gaze, Penny turns a saucy smile on me. "Just wait. Mine is after this one."

Mr. Barrett finishes up his discussion on the receding quality of cool colors and how any part of the anatomy painted this color will tend to draw back, no matter how strong the artist's intention is to make it protrude. I cringe.

He moves to scrutinize Penny's piece, massages his chin with his hand for a moment, and then spins around toward the expectant students perched on their drawing stools.

"If you'll remember, the assignment given was to take some aspect of human sexuality and communicate either a pro or con statement. Here," he gestures to Penny's piece. "We have a love letter to back door love."

Mr. Barrett's mouth twitches, and he looks at Penny while adjusting his glasses, as if seeing her for the first time. "Aside from an attempt to acquire more dates, I'm seeing that Miss Powell has endorsed the "pro" side of this ass-signment."

The entire class erupts in laughter that is a bit too loud.

Penny's lips quiver and her face grows livid, her fingers curl and uncurl, and she shakes on her high heels, something I've never seen happen before.

"Et tu, Barrett?" Penny steps forward, clutching her portfolio. "The pro side? What pro side?"

"The use of pink is quite positive." He nods.

"Positive!" Penny shouts. "Just once I'd like to go out with a guy who either doesn't want to do that or who has the guts to admit he wants to do that. You can't even discuss it without turning it into a joke." Penny's copper tresses shake. "Men want you to do that, but they don't want to talk about it. They're afraid it's gay. But they all want it. Look how many guys in this room are beet red right now."

"Now Penny—"

"And if I see one more proctologist joke on TV, I'm gonna puke."

She starts for the door. "You want to hear a joke I heard on the subway?" She cocks her head. "'What do you call a woman without an asshole?'" She pauses. "Single!"

No one laughs.

"Those are strong emotions." Mr. Barrett tugs on both ends of his scarf. "But I don't see any of them in your piece." He chuckles gently while the rest of the class hoots in hysterics.

"You DON'T GET IT. None of you GET IT." Penny stomps out of the room leaving her triple X-rated assignment pinned to the wall.

Absolute quiet descends.

It is Mr. Barrett's job to fill the void. "Art." He looks at the ceiling. "Can bring up powerful feelings. And sometimes pieces we're working on can subconsciously be about more than they appear, even to us, the artists."

I stare at the chalkboard in confusion. I've known Penny for years, but maybe I don't really know her at all. I assumed Penny to be worldly, sophisticated, cosmopolitan even. Penny takes everything in her long-legged stride. She doesn't have hang-ups.

Still, something about the instructor's glib attitude, and the male titters still circulating amongst the class, tell me Penny may have tapped into a vein too deep to mine.

"But why?" I become conscious that I've spoken out loud.

The German-intellectual glasses swivel my way. "Why what?"

"Oh, I'm sorry. I was just wondering. Penny told me on the way over here —well—she told me her piece was going to make you squirm. She wanted revenge for something that happened last week. So why did she make it all pink and pretty?"

In answer, a young man stands up. No, a woman, in buzzed black hair and leather jacket. "To heighten the hypocrisy, that's why. It's fucking brilliant." She turns to me. "You can't expect a man to be able to see the difference between that piece of art," she points, "and porno. Now in my opinion, that chick in the picture needs to be wearin' a strap-on. That'd be sayin' somethin'." She sits heavily. The chains on her jacket and buckles on her boots rattle and jingle.

Suddenly, due to time constraints, the instructor feels it necessary to move along to the next piece.

I want to leave. I'm not a legitimate student here. I should have left with Penny. It will be awkward and disruptive to get up now, especially after I've added to the discussion. I look at the holes in my shoes and wonder how long I should politely sit in the corner before leaving.

I escape at break, but not before I sneak over to the board, pull out the pushpins, and release Penny's porno into my custody.

The Admissions Office is at the bottom of the stairs. I stop in front of the big closed door. I hear Michael's voice in my head, calling me a loser. I go in.

After waiting behind several live bodies and several phone calls, suddenly nothing stands between me and the receptionist. With trepidation I approach the coiffed hair, perfect make-up, and arch expression of the woman behind the counter.

"Er, I'm looking for information on applying."

The woman touches her tongue to her top teeth and swivels in her office chair. "Do you mean you would like an application packet?"

"Yes."

An envelope, heavily stuffed, lands on top of the counter. I shift the cold café latte to the crook of my elbow, and pick up the packet with all the temerity of a squirrel accepting a nut from a human. Arms full, I back away from the counter. With thalidomide-defect movements I ease some of the paperwork from the envelope.

The number of zeroes at the end of the line marked tuition are staggering.

I clear my throat. "Excuse me. Are the financial aid or, er, the scholarship forms in here?"

The woman tosses another envelope onto the counter without looking up from her paperwork. As I move in to pick them up, my coffee cup tips and sticky caramel liquid pours over the counter and onto the woman's paperwork.

A whooshing vortex of air fills the room as she rises to her feet. In my rush to dab the spill with my snotty tissue, I drop Penny's painting on the carpet. The woman's mouth opens still further as her eyes fill with the contents of Penny's porno valentine.

Without a word, without looking at me, she points a finger at the door. I swallow hard. Those damn application papers cost me, there's no way I'm leaving them. I clutch the envelope to my chest, crushing the painting and the empty coffee cup, and flee.

CHAPTER FIFTEEN

New York City
March 17, 1981

Leave it to New York to throw a St. Patrick's Day parade, a
snowstorm, and a garbage strike all at once. The snows of February
seemed gone for good, until today. Warm and dry inside a delicatessen,
I finish the last few bites of my sandwich as I search out the windows
for X-It. We are to meet and watch the parade together.

Through the flurries, the throng of people, and the mounded bags
of garbage on the sidewalk, I spot him. His white-blond hair sticks out
from under his ski cap, pulled down as far as it can go. He is on foot.
Behind him are Voodoo, Pyro, Dogbite, the Mod Sisters, and Crikey.

I groan.

I've been doing so well at keeping X-It away from Voodoo that
this is a blow. X-It waves for me to join them, as naive as a toddler
who fell into the alligator exhibit. I swallow my last bit of sandwich,
shove my hands deep into my pockets, and rush outside.

"Crikey!" I exclaim. "What are you doing here? I thought you're
working on that fashion catalogue." My recommendation for the
modeling job at the mannequin factory has brought him good
connections and more jobs.

"Finished yester-dye. I'm signing with an agency next week."

"Bravo." I mentally hug myself.

With Voodoo in the lead and me in tow, the group makes an abrupt turn, like a school of sardines, toward Fifth Avenue and the parade. They squeeze ahead of me. Shut out, I swim along with the sea of humanity, engulfed in cologne and the smells of wet wool and stale beer. A snowflake falls on my nose.

As a group, we collect stares. The Mod Sisters belong uptown, like Sixties mannequins escaped from a storeroom. Pyro's flaming skull and Dogbite's mohawk clear us a place in front of the blue NYPD barricades.

Crikey turns back and smiles at me. "Come along then, Miss Buckingham. Don't let the parade pass you by."

I strain on my tiptoes to see above the crowd. Useless. I reach out my hand to find X-It's. He pulls me ahead with force and I remember how wiry he is. He pushes me in front of him and I am given the same privilege as New York's children, an unobstructed view of the parade. The press of people flattens X-It's body to mine. His breath, sweet and wheaty as a baby goat's, tickles my neck.

An overly polished uptown lady gives Voodoo an appreciative glance. Another woman, in her forties, smiles at him. My brow crinkles. There must be something about his gypsy-pirate exterior and boot-heeled swagger they find attractive.

I glance away to watch the police officers. Enormous police horses make me feel that much shorter. The mounts jingle and stamp, snort and steam, playing their role in the entertainment. The blocked off streets amaze me, the way it's even possible to shut down part of a city like New York.

The only time I've seen New York at a standstill was one night last month. X-It and I went to see Killing Joke at Dance-o-Matic. The show was good and having him all to myself was even better. It started to snow as we entered the club, and by the time we staggered into the street at three a.m., Manhattan lay under a quieting quilt of two feet of snow. It would be several hours before the city's snowplows woke up and went to work.

"X-It, it's magical!" I exclaimed, and ran right down the middle of Twenty-First Street, my army boots sinking into snow up past my knees. I turned south onto a mute Madison Avenue. The city was softened and sprinkled with glitter. Hard edges disappeared, and the usual pedestrian guideposts such as mailboxes and fire hydrants were unrecognizable sculptures.

A snowball hit me in the back of the head. I scooped my gloved hands into the white magic and flung it back at my very best friend. We were Peter Pan and Tinkerbelle on our very own island of Never Never Manhattan.

We crossed the Lower east Side on Sixth Street, X-It spotted a full dumpster and lithely dove in.

Teeth chattering, spell broken, I said, "Come on X, let's go, I'm cold."

His voice echoed from the dumpster, but I couldn't understand him. Minutes went by. I stood, cold and alone, on the sidewalk.

"X?" No answer. Shaking, I wondered if I should leave him and continue home. Just as I turned to go, his head reappeared.

"You'll never guess what I found. Look!" He hoisted a framed and mounted black and white poster of Andy Warhol.

"Cool. Let's go." I wanted to take his arm, but he carried the poster.

At our apartment, we opened the shutters and sat cross-legged on the floor in front of the windows, completely absorbed in the subtly changing colors wrought on each outdoor surface by the approaching sunrise. The snow-covered street acted as a dramatic blank canvas. I never knew so many colors of white existed.

Movement caught my eye. Emotion stuck in my throat. A junkie, dressed all in black, struggled weakly through the snowdrifts to reach the shooting gallery across the street. The pure and elegant beauty of the addict's negative form against the snow, fighting nature's opposition to her body's demands, made me cry.

Now at the parade, I grip the barricade. Blonde baton twirlers march by on pale, patchy-red legs. Why did X-It have to bring the drug addicts along? The St. Patrick's Day Parade seems little more than a procession of drums, cherry cheeks, and green satin banners straining across beer bellies. Perhaps it's my Scots genes handed down from Mim which aid my antipathy. My toes hurt from the cold and I want to leave.

I lean back my head and gaze up at X-It. "Let's go somewhere. Just you and me. How about going up to the top of the Empire State Building to see if this parade looks like a big green snake?"

"Nah, St. Patrick got rid of the snakes."

"Only in Ireland." I say, with a pointed look over at Voodoo. "Come on." I spin around, tug on the lapels of X-It's coat, and send him my very best Holly Golightly smile. "Let's go."

With our faces close and our bodies tight together, his features combine into an expression of distinct unease.

Green foil shamrocks rain down on us.

X-It pushes away from me and raises his hands palm upward, a delighted smile spreads across his face, it is the kind of seasonal theatric he would think of.

"Tra-La! Found you," sings out a throaty voice I have no trouble recognizing. Penny tosses another handful of shimmering shamrocks onto our motley group and poses, perfect in her slouchy suede boots and brown and white cowhide coat.

"Come with me, everybody," she announces, and holds up a shopping bag in her other hand. "In here is a shamrock cake, covered in green marzipan, and a bottle of Crème de Menthe. We are all going to the top of the Empire State Building for a proper St. Pat's!"

Damn.

I scuff at the sidewalk. I can't feel my toes. The green shamrocks shine up at me from the pavement, mocking my dullness. I contemplate going home, since all the dwarves are here, but I don't want to appear peevish. And besides, X-It knows going to the Empire State Building was my idea first, and he didn't think it a very good one at that. I tromp along as the group threads down the crowded Fifth

Avenue sidewalk to Thirty-Fourth Street, crossing against traffic signals, aided by the blue barricades that wall off the parade.

The second elevator that goes to the top of the Empire State Building always gives me difficulty. It's too small for the number of people in it, and I can't stop imagining the yawning distance stretched out below this little box strung up on cables.

Jeez, there isn't any air. I close my eyes.

A hand lands gently on my arm. X-It?

No. Voodoo.

"Are you alright?" His swirling brown irises appear genuinely concerned. "Come on." He takes my hand. "Count the floors with me as they light up."

Soon the entire elevator of people is counting the floors aloud. I begin to breathe more freely. The attendant, past retirement age, simply smiles.

The elevator doors open.

No one, not even a tourist in denial, is out on the observation deck. Penny pushes open the glass doors with abandon, as if she's an actress in a film. The rest of the group follows. Parade-side on Fifth Avenue is balmy compared to the frigid air a hundred and two stories up in the sky. The wind whips the flurries around and through the safety fencing. Penny walks upright, turns the corner, and settles herself along with the contents of the shopping bag, out of view of the doors and any nosy attendants.

X-It sits cross-legged beside her. X-It and Penny, King and Queen of St. Patrick's Day. Pyro, Dogbite, Crikey, and the Mod Sisters do the same. Voodoo squats down, balancing on the toes of his boots. I stand as close as I can to the building. I have no desire to look down, green-snake parade or not.

Slices of green cake are handed round, along with the bottle of sticky-sweet green alcohol. It's more like mouthwash than liqueur.

Penny holds her slice aloft, "Erin Go Bragh!"

"Erin go bra-less!" says Dogbite. The group laughs.

I butt my forehead against the wall, as if the pain will magically transport me away from here. I eat the cake layers first, saving the marzipan coating, my favorite, for last. This is difficult. My hands have joined my feet in numbness.

"I made this a special occasion to make a special announcement," says Penny. She takes a swig, which leaves her cherry red lips ringed in green, lending her a half-dead, fey quality. "I've found an apartment! It's a loft, actually. In SoHo, and it's so cool. It has floor-to-ceiling windows and concrete floors—you could roller skate—and industrial like steel beams. X-It's agreed to be partners with me on the lease, of course my parents co-signed, and all of you are welcome to come. Even you, J.J. —"

I whip around. "I have an apartment."

Stunned into shock beyond the cold, I wander to the fence near a pay telescope, but don't dare look down. I turn instead to look up at the spire, originally intended as a mooring for dirigibles. What a dumb and wonderfully fantastical idea that was.

I shiver. The spire looks too much like the hypodermic needle I found. Only this one is worthy of the God of all Junkies. I force a frigid breath. How can X-It be Penny's partner on her lease? X-It lives with me.

"Anyway, it's huge. I move in tomorrow." Penny jumps up and stuffs the empty cake box into the shopping bag. "Whoo! It's cold." She stamps her boots prettily. "Let's all go see my new place."

* * *

My footsteps echo, along with the others', in Penny's cavernous new digs. The rest of my body is now as deadened as my hands and feet. I want to go home and go to sleep so I don't have to think or feel.

"How can he do this to me?" I scream inside my head. I trace a finger along mortar lines in the wall of exposed brick, half hoping a sharp edge will cut it.

"Ow." I get my wish.

X-It comes over. "You better wash that. I'll show you where the bathroom is. There're *two* of them."

He flips on the switch for me. "Isn't this place the coolest?" He smiles. "Do you like it?"

I frown, this is the kind of place only well-established artists can afford. Penny's life doesn't have to follow the same rules as most other people's lives.

"X-It," calls Penny at the top of her voice from the partial second story, "Let's figure out whose room is whose."

He leaves to join her.

Crikey and Voodoo appear in the doorway of the bathroom as I hunt for any kind of paper product to blot my finger. There is none.

"Nice crapper," says Crikey. "I'll be moving out too, ya know." He catches my eye.

"Why wouldn't you be?" I scowl.

"What I mean is, I won't be coming here. I've found a place closer to Seventh Avenue on the Upper West Side, with a bunch of male models from the agency—"

Voodoo sniggers.

Crikey ignores him. "Thanks, J.J. girl, for everything."

He looks from me to Voodoo with a strange expression riding his features, then turns and leaves.

Voodoo slides into the bathroom and gently takes my hand. He guides it over the sink.

"It's best to flush it out," he says, squeezing the cut until drops of blood show on the curving porcelain. He continues to wring blood out of my finger by rolling it between his own. He then dips the tip of his index finger in my blood as it's about to drip, and paints a sensuous streak up the underside of my arm.

"So red." His breath warms my ear. "There's something sexy about blood, don't you think?"

Our eyes meet in the mirror. I feel faint and wobble. Suddenly he is all competent business.

"Let's wash that." He holds my finger under the running tap and then dries it by squeezing it with a hanky drawn with a flourish from his back pocket. He wipes off my arm.

He examines the red stains on the white hanky, kisses them with eyebrows raised like a vaudeville Don Juan, mocking his own image, and then stuffs it back in the rear pocket of his black jeans.

"Come on, I'll get you home."

I take Voodoo's elbow. I can't bear to say good-bye to X-It. I might start yelling. Might throw things. I look around the pristine loft. There is nothing here to throw. I might hit him. With my fists.

Tears won't come. Thank God they're as frozen as my feet. They'll come later when I defrost.

Voodoo escorts me, mostly in silence, across Manhattan to the Lower East Side and home. My fingers still frozen, one pulsing from the cut, I hand him the keys to my apartment.

He turns the lock, opens the door by giving it a small shove, and then says, "I'm not moving in with Penny."

"Your business," I say, wanting to go lie down.

"I'm glad to hear you say that. I'm staying here."

"No!" My reaction is instinctive and immediate.

He touches my arm. "You'll need someone to take over X-It's share of the rent. I'll pay a hundred dollars more a month than he did."

I think of my bank account. I don't have enough to cover all of the rent if X-It leaves. He did leave. Without even considering me. Damn him.

The tears threaten to come now. Damn them.

Voodoo fully enters the apartment. I lean against the door as it shuts.

"Do you think," I blearily try to focus on Voodoo's face. "If I'd put X-It's name on the lease, made him partner, do you think he would've stayed?"

Voodoo puts his arm around my shoulder, pulls me away from the door to lean on him, and says, "I think you'd be in a worse situation than you are now."

He's being so nice. I sink into him and let the tears come.

"With things this way," he continues in soothing tones, "It's still your apartment. You've got control."

CHAPTER SIXTEEN

New York
April, 1981

I return from doing my laundry, alone. I set down my pillowcase of clean clothes and run to answer the ringing phone.

Voodoo gets there before me. "It's for you. A man."

I take the receiver and dismiss him with waves of my hand. He play-sulks as far as the kitchen then spins to stare at me. I turn away.

"Michael! Good to hear you."

"How are you J.J.? I've been a little concerned. I haven't heard from you."

"Sorry." I wipe my nose. "I'm not so good. I didn't want to call you in yet another crisis. You must think I'm such a flake."

"What's going on?"

"Penny and most of the dwarves are gone. Trouble is, she took X-It with her." My voice starts to choke. "He's my best friend."

"Can't you still be friends and live in separate apartments? All of my friends do. Art doesn't count." He chuckles. "What'd you mean, most of the dwarves?"

"Voodoo's still here," I whisper.

Michael's voice, usually so mellow and down to earth, acquires an edge. "The drug dealer?"

"He's being really nice to me."

The tension in his voice to rises a couple of notches. "You're alone with this guy?"

"At separate ends of the apartment. He bailed me out by taking over X-It's rent."

"I hope you know what you're doing."

"Hah." I twine the phone cord around my arm. I watch as my skin turns blotchy and my veins pop out.

"Did you check out art school?"

"Um-hmm. Disaster."

Silence takes over. I swear I can hear his disappointment.

He says, "Take care, J.J. Call me if you're in trouble."

"Yeah. Sure."

*   *   *

The doorbell rings. I open it to find Russ, the Dance-o-Matic assistant manager. He called yesterday to ask me out for my nineteenth birthday, and I couldn't think of a good enough reason to turn him down.

"Are you ready? You're hair isn't purple anymore."

"Er, yes. And no, it isn't."

Voodoo appears behind me, dressed to kill. "We're going to Dance-o-Matic then?" He runs his hand down his front, smoothing his brocade waistcoat.

Russ sucks in his chin for a moment, his eyes wide. He recovers and says, "Yeah, why not?"

I discover I don't really mind if Voodoo tags along. A threesome might hinder Russ's objective for the evening. I'm not in the mood to tolerate his advances.

And I desperately do not want to run into Penny and X-It at Dance-o-Matic, so I say, "Russ, you don't want to go to the office on your night off, let's go to Sphinx."

"Fine." His Rockabilly swoop bobs in agreement. "It's closer, anyway." He links arms with mine, and Voodoo hovers near my other elbow the entire short distance to the nightclub.

The door to Sphinx remains closed during business hours, which adds to the club's mystery. Through this portal layered in scabbed paint and New York history, we enter the tiniest, darkest, and trendiest nightspot in town. I don't know the bartender by name but by sight. I like him, gently spoken, tall, always polite to short people. I know he comes to work here from a mostly black area of Brooklyn.

With a hesitant smile, I disengage from my twofold escort and begin my approach to the crowded bar in a manner not unlike a grain of sand in an hourglass. In time, my sternum presses against the bar rail. I moisten my lips in preparation to order. The bartender's friendly grin and jaunty mini-dreads turn in my direction. I stand on my toes.

"Three beers, please." I slide the money.

His gaze rises along with his eyebrows as he looks from the three beers, to me, to my double dates. He passes back my change with a sly wink. Heat flushes my face. I leave the money on the bar. This is X-It's fault. He left me at the mercy of Russ and Voodoo. I grind my teeth, then let out a seething breath between them. How can he do this to me? How can he manage to humiliate me and not even be present? Tipping back my beer, I drink half of it in one go.

Russ, as assistant manager at Dance-o-Matic, carries clout in the club world. We soon find ourselves seated at one of the few tables. Smoke hangs heavy in the air. In his best James Dean manner, Russ taps a cigarette out of its box.

"May I have one?" I'm a poser smoker, only engaging in the activity in moments of extreme social tension.

"Sure baby," says Russ out the side of his mouth, his unlit cancer stick moves up and down with his words. He brings my cigarette to red glowing life with a flourish of his lighter.

Voodoo laughs. His fingers protrude beneath lace cuffs—a bit Jim Morrison, a bit Captain Hook—and tap upon the little black box he always carries with him. He excuses himself to go to the gents'.

I squint to watch his form eel its way through the crowd, finish my beer, and then ask Russ for another. Alone at the table, my side aches as if someone has taken a machete and severed me from my Siamese twin. Knowing X-It is uptown having fun without me makes everything hollow. The music reverberates like I'm in a barrel, not a nightclub.

I close my eyes. Russ returns. I open my eyes to see two beers and two sidecar shots of tequila. My nose fills with the biting smells of smoke and alcohol.

Both glasses are drained by the time Voodoo exits the restroom. He wipes his nose with his knuckles and turns to speak to someone behind him. It's Sheila, Mod Sister number one.

What's she doing here? She never breaks orbit with Planet Penny and the Mindless Asteroids and so by all rights should be at Dance-o-Matic.

Sheila and Voodoo edge onto the miniscule dance floor, already writhing with bodies, and move to *The Tide is High*. Russ pulls me from my seat. Dancers sway, came together and drift apart. Flashes of faces and bodies go by.

White hair, full lips. Copper hair, long legs. X-It. And Penny.

Blondie sings.

Barely conscious of it, I ball my fists. I cut through dancers like a hot knife through ice cream.

X-It recognizes me and smiles his wide puppy dog smile. I smash my fist into his face.

The room isn't big enough for so many bodies to maneuver out of the way as X-it flies backward. My feet lift from the floor as Russ grabs one of my elbows and Voodoo the other.

The music stops. Lights come on.

The friendly bartender flings a towel down and jumps over the bar. He separates patrons who were accidentally hit by X-It and are now itching for a fight.

I throw my head back and laugh. All club goers stand frozen, stark in the glare, stripped of their cool and made ridiculous by the lack of music and atmosphere. We're all absurd. Me most of all.

X-It stares at me from the floor with the accusing eyes of a slapped infant. Horrified. Betrayed. Scared.

I look away.

"I'm sorry. You three will have to leave," says the bartender.

"Why me?" asks Russ, letting go of my elbow.

Voodoo accepts my weight, adding his other hand to my waist.

The jaunty mini-dreads of the bartender shake at me, but his eyes hold something like wry respect. "Because you're with her," he says to Russ.

Outside Sphinx's closed portal, Russ isn't ready to call it a night. "Let's go up to Dance-o-Matic. There's some paperwork I should check on."

"On your night off?" I ask. I'm drunk.

I wrinkle my nose at him. He had his status insulted by being asked to leave and now wishes to restore it by acting The Man at Dance-o-Matic.

"No rest for the wicked." He slicks back his swoop with a comb then pushes it perfectly into place without the aid of a mirror.

Voodoo slides his hand across my back. "What would you like to do?"

My mind reels. I hit X-It. "I don't know. I'll leave it up to you."

"You've had quite a shock. I'll be wherever you are. You shouldn't be alone tonight." Voodoo strokes my arm.

Russ breaks in loudly, "What was that all about in there, J.J.? Are you sleeping with that guy you decked?"

"No."

"Is he sleeping with the girl he was dancing with?"

"No." At least I don't think so.

"You mean to tell me you punched a guy you never slept with, for dancing with a girl he never slept with?"

My face lowers. I blew it. Michael's words come back to me, "Can't you still be friends and live in separate apartments?"

But X-It and I were more than friends. He is lost to me. His hurt expression haunts my mind.

"You wouldn't understand."

"Are we dating or aren't we?" He moves to grab my shoulders but Voodoo is in the way.

I stiffen, rubbing my sore knuckles. "That depends on whether you want a girlfriend or a roadie."

"What?"

"I don't carry guitars."

He still appears confused. "You're a screwy chick. I'm going to D-land. Come along if you want to." He starts down the street then stops and turns. "Are you sleeping with this guy?" He points to Voodoo.

"No."

"Well doesn't that make me the lucky one? Come on let's catch a cab."

I whisper to Voodoo, "He's not gonna get lucky tonight."

"Maybe not," he smiles, exposing wolfish teeth. "But he can get us in for free."

Russ makes sure we're well aware of this fact once we arrive at Dance-o-Matic. He tells us to wait out front for him, he'll go in the back and come round to let us in. It's his way of telling me I'm dependent upon him for any social status and that sleeping with him would be in my best interest. Yuck. Why can't I be like Penny and make my own status?

The DJ with the shoulder length black hair who played The Sleepers for me is pulling a stint in the ticket booth.

When Voodoo and I approach he asks, "You're Russ's Elvis painter, right?"

At the moment I don't desire to be Russ's anything, but don't want to give up the free entry into the club. I hold out my hand. "I'm J.J. Buckingham."

"Todd Carruthers, otherwise known as Hot Toddy."

Russ is nowhere in sight. How long does he expect us to wait outside? Thank goodness Todd recognizes me.

Hot Toddy waves us in. "I'll be back in the booth in a half hour. Come keep me company on the second floor. You two look really bitchin'. When I start things up, why don't you dance and get people to come out on the floor?"

I blanch at the thought.

A bangled wrist flops down on my shoulder and Voodoo's teeth flash near my cheek. He answers for me, "She'd love to come up and dance. See you later."

Todd grins.

Voodoo and I sit safely ensconced in a Neo-Retro Naugahyde booth on the third floor.

"That tequila I had earlier was good," I say.

"I'll buy you a shot," Voodoo says and sets down his black leather box near his feet.

I accept. Voodoo buys me two more.

He leans his elbows on the table and smiles at me. "You should go for it."

"For what?"

"That scrumptious DJ."

"He doesn't like me."

"Blind and stupid." He laughs and comes closer. His breath smells of spearmint. "You should go for everything. For Life. For the brass ring. You're so close." He traces his finger along my cheekbone; his bracelets rattle along his arm. "And so beautiful."

I jump at his touch, remembering this is Voodoo.

"Why are you being so," I can't think of the word. "So supportive?"

"J.J., I can be your best friend."

I'm in need of a new one.

"I've known you a long time," he continues. "I can give you everything you want. I can make you shine brighter than a new copper penny."

It is clear to whom he refers.

He continues, "I can make you clever, outgoing. I can take away your fear. I can give you the DJ. I can give you any man you want." His eyes glitter as he pauses. "I can give you X-It."

After my third shot of tequila, this all sounds pretty good. "How?"

"You have to want me to. Do you want me to?"

I gaze into his swirling eyes. I see myself dancing, more charismatic than Penny, attracting all club patrons onto the dance floor like moths so they can be near my brightness. I see X-It tossing a sock at me, laughing, doing laundry together again.

"Yes," I croak, "Oh, yes."

He orders two more shots of tequila then reaches down and puts the black box on his lap. From a small vial he taps two thin lines onto the triangular top of his fist. He takes a short straw from his waistcoat pocket and snorts the powder.

"Bottoms up," he says.

Should I? Never again do I want to be a pathetic girl holding guitars out in the snow. Our glasses clink together in a toast and I down the shot. I look from his smile to the line of powder. He's still alive. I shrug, slide to his side of the booth, pick up the straw, and bend my nose to his hand.

Nothing happens.

"I suggest you go to the second floor now. I'm right behind you." He packs up.

"Okay." I'm a little wobbly from all that tequila in such a short space of time. Halfway down the stairs a rush of blood hits the back of my throat and I cough. My feet decide to bounce up the steps and I feel like dancing.

Hot Toddy is in the DJ booth, wearing headphones and moving to the groove. More than my feet feel like dancing, every molecule vibrates with the music. I spin over to Todd and flash him a brilliant smile.

He gives me a thumbs up and reaches for the microphone, "Disco is dead, folks, so let's have a requiem. Here's K.C. and the Sunshine Band."

The second floor club patrons aren't quite sure what to make of this development; Disco may be dead but the body is still warm. The floor clears. Uncertain of what to do, I smile blankly at everyone.

Voodoo is at my side in a blink, his hand in mine, his black-heeled boots moving with precision as the song pumps out a strong beat. I follow him. He's a tremendous dancer. What fun!

The dance floor fills. The D.J. is pleased.

The magic lasts for a couple of hours. I talk to complete strangers and every word out of my mouth sparkles with wit. I speak right up and laugh out loud. Everyone appears to be captivated by me. I lap it up.

Voodoo grins down at me. He's so much taller than X-It. "Your pupils are huge," He says. "They make your eyes look so sexy."

"Really?"

"Yeah."

I stumble with dizziness and he leads me into a booth. "Wow. I'm flagging." I laugh weakly. "Can you make me the Belle of the Ball again?" X-It should see me, I think with a pang.

"I can do that, but J.J., you're going to have to trust me."

Trust Voodoo? But I want to shimmer full blast again, want everyone to acknowledge my magnificence.

What the hell. This is only for tonight. "What do I do?"

"Go in the women's bathroom on the fourth floor and sit in the middle stall, I'll be right up."

Being recognized as a girl Russ sometimes dates gives me full fourth floor privileges. I enter the restroom then wait patiently in the middle stall. A tap signals Voodoo's arrival. He slips inside with his black box.

"Get up."

I comply. He sits on the toilet and pulls me down onto his lap. I start to protest. He puts his finger to his lips, admonishing me to be silent. The open black box he places on my lap. He taps a small amount of crystalline powder into a large spoon then drops a tiny wad of cotton onto it. He uncaps a syringe and sucks up what looks like water from another vial.

I squirm. "I'm not doing heroin."

He claps a hand over my mouth. "Shhh. It's crystal. The same stuff you did a couple of hours ago."

I relax a bit, about as much as a racehorse in the starting gate waiting for the other horses to be loaded. This is my doorway to becoming the J.J. I really want to be. The J.J. who can charm X-It. He shoots the water into the spoon and waits for the powder to dissolve then sticks the needle in the cotton and draws the liquid into the syringe.

"What are you going to do with that?" I ask as he taps the side of the hypodermic to remove air bubbles.

"Just what you think I'm going to do."

"It's not clean." I start to panic. "You don't have any alcohol."

Voodoo chuckles, "Type A J.J. For you, my princess, I used a brand new one. It came out of the sterile package moments ago."

There is no way out but full speed ahead. "Voodoo…I— "

"Shh shh shh." He holds me close, ensuring the box and its contents do not spill. "Remember the first time you had sex? This is no different. And I'm very good."

"I've never enjoyed sex."

"Poor you." His lips pucker in sympathy. "I can take care of that later. But right now I guarantee you're going to enjoy this. Let me show you, J.J."

"Do it." I want to squeeze my eyes shut but can't stop watching.

After setting the box on the floor, he slips his belt around my upper arm, tightens it, and tells me to hold the end taut. He taps two fingers against the inside of my arm.

"You've got fabulous veins," he says, the same way another man might comment on my breasts. "You're in shape."

"I run."

"Not from me anymore." The needle bites into my blood vessel without pain. A blush of blood shows in the syringe and he pushes the plunger to its limit. "Happy birthday, J.J."

I experience something quite akin to losing my virginity, only this is much sexier. There is penetration. There is blood. But then comes a tidal wave of pleasure. Like the space shuttle Columbia on its recent flight test, I launch into takeoff. I buck and arch backward against him. Voodoo runs his hands up and down the front of me. His touch is delicious.

My vision is ringed with crystalline, kaleidoscopic rainbows, and I can perceive the inherent divine splendor in every goddamn thing, even the toilet.

"Oh my God. Oh my God. Oh my God."

CHAPTER SEVENTEEN

At six a.m. on Fifth Street between Avenue A and B, the limo pulls to the litter-strewn curb, the door opens and out stretches my dainty foot clad in an army boot.

"I gave my number to sooo many people!" I trill and fall back against Voodoo with a laugh. He thanks the driver, who was provided by the host of the after hours party. No less than three different people invited me. Three! Not even Penny gets invited to this kind of party. I swear I saw Jody Foster. *And* the unmistakable personage of Andy Warhol.

Wait until I tell—

I stumble up the step. Voodoo takes my arm. In my room, alone, I sink upon the chaise. I push thoughts of X-It away, using the memories of all the people I chatted with last night, all the people who looked in my eyes and were intrigued with what they saw there.

Voodoo knocks. What does he want? He approaches with his palm upward, cradling a white pill.

"You're not going to sleep unless you take this. Trust me, it'll be much better if you take it."

He's always asking me to trust him. Last night worked out pretty well. More than pretty well. I pick up the pill and read the letters embossed on it.

"Q-u-a-a-l-u-d-e. What's that mean?"

"It means it wasn't made in someone's garage and that I'm being very generous. I'm off to shower. See you this afternoon."

I go to the kitchen to get some water to swallow the tablet then return to my room. My hand hesitates before locking the deadbolt, but I lock it.

After removing my boots and dress I lie down and gather the blankets about me. My finger traces the tiny red dot and bruise nestled in the crook of my elbow. As my eyelids grow heavy, I think I see the candles held aloft by mannequin arms come alight. But that can't be.

*   *   *

New York
May, 1981

The doorbell rings again. I flit over to answer it.

"Monica! James! Eduardo! Welcome to my humble downtown digs."

My party is in full swing and my apartment is crowded. I take their coats and jostle to allow them room to come through the door.

"Drinks are in the kitchen," I say to my new guests. "Kenny and Chantal are already here."

James, Monica, and Eduardo—a quasi-famous fashion illustrator—make their way to the kitchen through the throng, and I take up court once more in front of the fireplace. I clamp my teeth onto my long black cigarette holder and pull up elbow-length black gloves along my twiggy arms to make sure they cover my track marks.

"As I was saying," I resume my conversation with an independent filmmaker, who teaches at NYU, and his devotees, "Each of my mother's successive boyfriends is missing a body part."

Laughter tinkles amid the clink of wine glasses and Brian Eno's *Music For Airports*.

"Ralph in Tucson was missing an ear and part of his jaw." I point the mouth end of the cigarette holder to each corresponding area of anatomy. "Tucker in Seattle was amputated below the elbow. Ken in Boulder below the knee. Her last one was missing fingers in Encinitas. But this guy…" I return the holder to my mouth, pick up my mother's latest postcard and then tap it on the mantle. "I can't see anything missing, from the photo." I silently read my mother's writing, *Me and Martin in Moss Beach, CA.* "Could be he's all there?"

"Might be a eunuch," offers the filmmaker.

A round of guffaws issues from his groupies.

Fleeting discomfort outwits the guardians of my chemically enhanced personality. I reach for an hors d'oeuvre to cover my distress, remember food tastes awful, and spit it delicately into a tissue.

Has my mother progressed to a whole man?

That magnitude of growth and healing shames my reduction of my mother's life into the kind of clever banter that will impress a SoHo-ite. Hell, I even imagined my quips about my mother's boyfriends showing up in an art film a year or two from now.

"You should paint them," says Max, a forty-ish and very female owner of an art gallery on St. Mark's Place. Max wears a bustier and black lace gloves, like that girl who hangs out at Dance-o-Matic, but she left off the crucifix and added purple mascara. Max's gallery is one of a group of downtown galleries.

"Paint who? My mother's boyfriends?" I take an actual puff from my cigarette in its holder.

"It'd make one helluva series." Max raises her glass.

It's already one helluva real life series.

"But," I smile impishly. "Wouldn't that be a departure from the Mad Dog and Dead Baby School of Painting?"

Max spits a mouthful of wine back into her glass. "What?"

All ears are on me.

"Most of the paintings I see in Lower East Side galleries are sure to include either a mad dog, a dead baby, or both." I smile again.

Max cocks her head to one side, a quizzical expression on her face. Those around her hold their breath.

Max's features crumple and her mighty bosom swells like waves against the inadequate jetty of her bustier as she surrenders to a fit of hilarity. Her laugh infects the room. Glasses are raised.

I'm the toast of the town.

As the laughter quiets to a normal level of conversation, I look to the stack of my paintings in the corner. I haven't painted since my Transformation.

No matter.

I could use topping off. I hop from the fireplace hearth and go to find Voodoo in the back bedroom where he generally conducts business when I throw a party. He enjoys the higher level of clientele. They pay up front.

Voodoo's room resembles a boudoir for a Gypsy Vampire. I pull back the fringed tablecloth that hangs slantwise in the doorway and enter. He even drapes gauzy scarves over a peculiar lighting fixture he's fond of, a pointy, star-shaped, glass creation.

Even though there are others in the room, I walk up and throw my arms around his neck, about which he wears a necklace of real tiger teeth. As I kiss him, I sense the envy in the other men there.

"Any chance of a pick-me-up?"

"Walk this way." He hams, and holds open the door to a small walk-in closet that serves as his nurse's station. I move aside more scarves and sit on a beat-up black wooden stool, his black leather case is next to it. The heavy scent of patchouli hangs in the air, cut only by the fresh mint of his breath as he leans over me, his necklace of teeth grazing my forehead.

When I'm properly soaring again he asks me, "Stay here, in my room, tonight?"

It won't be the first time.

I toss back my head and giggle, knowing he finds my throat irresistible.

"Maybe." I flash my eyes at him and flutter away, trailing my fingers. Any upper hand over Voodoo is intoxicating. I take three steps into the living room, lit by the chili-pepper palm trees, and stop dead.

This is no mannequin. The real Karisma poses, and smiles, and lifts her glass to drink, and breathes the air—in my apartment.

Thank goodness for Voodoo and his little pick-me-ups. I float up to the celebrated young model, black-gloved fingers extended, and introduce myself. On the inside, I hop up and down like a little girl. Karisma. At my party.

The doorbell rings again. I tear myself away from Karisma's admittedly less than riveting conversation and answer the door. Penny, and X-It.

With what I hope is an indiscernible cover-up for my momentary shock, I launch into a wave of niceties that swamp even Penny, "Oh how are you? Haven't seen you in so long. How is that great big loft of yours? And good old Professor Barrett?"

I do not, cannot, look at X-It.

Penny crashed my party.

My magnanimity extends to allowing them entrance to my party, but not so far as introducing them around. I return to the group of people that include Max and the filmmaker, and spend most of the remainder of the evening trying to ignore X-It. Once in a while I look up and catch sight of him. Well, okay, every chance I get, but I try not to let him see me.

"That young man looks at you a good deal," says Max, gesturing with her wine glass toward X-It.

I crinkle my nose. "I can't think why." Because he can't believe how popular I've made myself. Without him. I try to scratch my nose with gloved fingers and the cigarette holder falls to the ground. My cheeks burn. I may be dressed like Holly Golightly, but it is X-It who is most like her. And I am caught, in love with a wild thing.

Retrieving the holder, I return to a conversation in full swing amongst the filmmaker and his followers concerning the merits of John Waters in particular and shock value in general. I add a few confectionary sprinkles on top of the discussion here and there but my mind is on the ghost of my dear departed bosom buddy as he appears, disappears, and reappears among my guests.

Later, I see him speaking to Eduardo.

I smile. Excellent. Now there's a good contact for him. X-It can draw rings around Eduardo's work, and deserves to share in the same kind of success. My eyelids spasm. Tears threaten, but my ducts are dry from all the speed. It seems I cannot hold on to my anger where X-It is concerned. I excuse myself and head to the bathroom to check my mascara. After closing the door, I realize I'm not alone. The unmistakable sound of vomiting comes from the bathtub.

I step closer and look down. Karisma is on all fours, looking less than glamorous. I do what any member of the sisterhood would do in that situation and hold back her hair.

"A bit too much to drink?"

Karisma finishes and lolls back into a sitting position; a goofy expression distorts her beauty.

"Not at all. I feel great. That gypsy guy has got some good stuff. Hand me that washcloth, will you?"

All of Karisma's long bones appear to have gone rubbery. "Yeah. He gets the best crystal," I agree.

"Crystal? That stuff is for bikers and trailer trash, and besides, it'll make you look old really fast."

Karisma finishes wiping her face and I extend my hand to help her out of the tub.

"Cocaine?" I ask.

"Way too disco."

"So what did he give you then?"

"He gave me nothing. I paid for the best heroin you can get in this stupid city." She leans toward the mirror and inspects her teeth. To me it seems as if my mannequin's head floats in space.

"You," Karisma points at me in the mirror, "are invited to my party next Friday night, and bring the gypsy."

* * *

In the shadowy patchouli-stink of Voodoo's room, I nestle against him in his brass bed, my eyes wide open. I marvel that I used to think him evil. He needs the comfort of a warm human body at the end of the day like anyone else. But Karisma's words give rise to doubts. Trailer trash? Does Voodoo think I'm not worth giving heroin?

I cast my mind over the promises he made. He gave me Manhattan. Can I have any man I want? Who knows? But I don't want just any man. I want X-It.

I sleep with Voodoo once or twice a week because it's inevitable. He's wrong about himself though. I can tell he's an accomplished lover, light years ahead of Russ, but so far I experience no more pleasure with him than in any of my previous sexual encounters, which confirms my deficiency. But I do enjoy this type of closeness, his sleepy head on my chest, where he seems to need me.

Voodoo embraces me like he embraces Darkness. He toys with it, braids it, and winds it around his finger as he lowers himself into it's depths. He requires my physical presence as insurance, a lifeline back to the mouth of the cave. This vulnerability, more than anything else, is what captures my adherence.

I prod him. "Voo- wake up."

"Unngh."

"Why won't you let me do heroin?"

"Junk?" He opens one eye. "I thought you just admired junkies from afar. Being a junkie's not all it's cracked up to be, you know."

"If Karisma can do heroin, I can do heroin." I pout. "Besides, why were you always chasing me to do heroin in San Francisco?"

"I changed my mind." He's fully awake now and leans over me, his curly black tendrils tickle my collarbone. "Any fool can see that all you needed was a little boost to have everyone eating out of your hand. Crystal was the ticket, trust me." He flops onto his back.

"I want to do heroin."

"No," he says with an authority that pisses me off. " It will make you dull. And you need to knock off the speed too. You don't need it anymore."

I'm not sure I want to be on that mythic plane alongside Jim and Janis, but I am sure I don't want Voodoo telling me what I can't do.

I tap the upside-down pentacle pendant, which hides in his black chest hair like an Easter egg. "That's a very old symbol you know. It's got nothing to do with Satan. Why do you wear it?"

He grabs me and pulls me close. His irises swirl. "Because it scares people."

My wrist hurts. "Ow. Let go."

"There's so much fear built up around this." He touches the necklace. "All I have to do is wear it to draw the fear out of people, use it against them. Fear makes people…manageable." He lets me go and grins.

I rub my wrist.

I ask him, "Did you name yourself Voodoo?"

He grabs me again, this time in a friendly hug and pulls me to the mattress. "Are you kidding? Dogbite and Pyro dubbed me. Back in the early days. Christ, I think it was the eighth grade. It stuck."

"What's your real name?"

He hesitates, then speaks, "Marko. I come from a long family line of black magi- er, sheep."

I sit up. He pulls me back down.

"We're Romany, originally from Czechoslovakia, but my grandparents were asked to leave, and most of us are California auto mechanics now."

I suppress an inappropriate giggle, born of truth in absurdity. His eyes sober me quickly.

"Darkness is just the other side of the coin," he explains. "Night and Day. There is no wholeness, no balance, without the other. There's nothing to be afraid of," he touches my face, "as long as you're willing to look at it. Look at me J.J."

"I'm looking at you, Marko." I put my arms around Voodoo. We are light and dark, two halves of a whole. As I lay my head on his chest, I have to acknowledge his power. But I know he's not all-powerful. He hasn't brought me X-It.

Later, I leave for work. I look at the ground as I descend the front stairs. The weather is getting warm enough to soften gum on the sidewalk.

A huge guy steps into my path and I try to sidestep around him. He shadows me. I look up. Shit, his eyes, void of moral ambiguity, tell me I'm his target.

His leather vest tells me he's a member of the motorcycle gang whose headquarters is down on Third Street. He says, "Is this where the Gypsy lives?"

"Who?" I ask, shaken.

But his grin is tight and malicious as he registers the confirmation in my face. "You tell the Gypsy to go back where he came from. Today."

I stare.

"You tell him. And just to make sure you do, you can let him know it wouldn't take much to break your little arms."

My mouth opens.

"Got it, Girly?"

I gurgle a response, and he leaves.

CHAPTER EIGHTEEN

New York
June, 1981

I did as I was told. Voodoo laughed. I think about the threat from time to time. Mostly, I miss X-It. I haven't seen him since my party.

As I rinse out a hypodermic under the tap, I wonder what he's doing. I now refer to them as "works," borrowing the parlance of the drug world. I've used this needle three or four times already. It's getting dull and that hurts. Taking my nail file to the tip is tempting, but Voodoo cautioned me against doing that before he left town. Little bits of metal can end up in your bloodstream. Not good.

In his paternally toned lecture he also warned me about overshooting the vein, going in one side and right out the other, delivering crystal into fleshy tissue, which will cause a nasty abscess. His homily was punctuated with graphic "real-life" horror stories, not unlike driver's ed. And then he left, business trip he called it. He handed me the rent money, a new postcard from my mother that came in the mail, a few works, some speed and a couple of 'ludes, and said he'd be back in two weeks.

That was three weeks ago. I half hope he comes back, and half hope he stays away.

My mother's postcard is from Vancouver, but she and Martin haven't moved there, they're just on vacation. A vacation postcard. Is Carla attaining normalcy?

She writes that they're having a good time and were sure to buy the extra insurance on the rental car as Martin has poor depth perception on account of his glass eye.

Disgusted and strangely let down, I throw the postcard away.

Damn Voodoo. How can he leave me alone? He should have been back a week ago. It's just me and the mannequin arms left in the apartment now. Except sometimes I think I see the shadowy long-haired hippy-witch woman. Whenever I see her I smell lavender.

I startle, shocked at the thought that I'm not completely alone. I have my drugs.

Do I have enough? Sudden fear grips my guts. My shallow breaths flutter my nostrils like a deer's, sniffing for danger, always flight, never fight. I search in my purse for my special compact, find it, and click the latch open with a trembling fingernail. My crystal is low, maybe two more doses. I scratch my forehead. This is not good.

Marko, Marko, are you coming back?

Arrhythmia rolls my heart over in my chest like a somersaulting bullfrog. Cramps bite the back of my calves. When was the last time I drank a glass of water? Maybe I should start taking vitamins again?

I have to get more speed.

The phone rings. Michael. His monthly call. Who does he think he is? My big brother?

"I'm fine, really," I answer his predictable prattle. A sliver of guilt works its way forward. I frown.

"You don't sound fine."

"I'm fine, fine, fine, fine, fine."

"Good." He takes a huge sucking breath I can hear from three thousand miles away, and then speaks, letting it all out in a rush, "J.J., I mean this, if you ever need a place to come to, a safe place, come stay with me."

Silence.

"Fine." I disconnect.

The Sphinx. My thoughts whirl. Hot Toddy said he'd be at Sphinx tonight. He'll have some speed, or know who does. I put the finishing styling touches on midnight blue hair tinged in red, it hangs forward over one eye in a sinister fashion. It suits me and I know it. The phone rings again and I answer the caller.

"Hi Karisma. The Gypsy's still out of town." I stretch the phone cord into the bathroom.

"Darn," she says. The model's voice is so ordinary when not attached to her face. "Well come to my party anyway. You always liven things up. I heard a rumor Warhol might show."

"Fab," I say sarcastically. Exasperated, I make a demon face then snarl into the mirror. Shit, my eyes are bloodshot. I open the cabinet and reach for the eye drops.

"Oh, do come," pleads Karisma.

Suddenly the idea of being outside of my apartment seems too ominous to bear. Forces gather against me. If I can stay under the streetlights I might be okay. It's the thought of getting safely from streetlight to streetlight that terrifies me. The dark in between might swallow me up.

I say shakily, "I don't know."

"Oh please come. Do you really know Crikey Madison, that mega-hot Aussie? I saw him on a shoot and he said he knows you. Boy, you just know everybody. He'll be here. Come on."

Shame lowers its silk veil across my face. I blow it away with deep red lips. I should go. To see Crikey.

"I'll come if I can," I answer with truth, and hope I can make it to Sphinx. I hang up, and just make it back to the bathroom when the phone rings again.

I sigh with irritation, such is the life of a social butterfly. Somebody should gas me and pin me to black velvet.

"Hello," I say with an edge, pulling the phone cord around the bathroom doorjamb.

"Hey-ya, it's Russ."

He probably wants me to show up at D-land and add some cachet to the place.

"To what do I owe this honor?" Looking again in the mirror, I rub my teeth with my finger. My gums feel weird.

"I'm uptown at a recording studio with Generika. We've booked it for the evening. You should come down. Er, up."

"I don't know." I shake with fear at the thought of getting in a cab.

"Oh come on, we're having fun. I haven't seen you in awhile." His voice turns away from the phone. "Geez! Parker, get a rag." He returns to his conversation with me, laughing. "The singer just spilled his beer down the console. I gotta go. Come on over. Please." He gives me the street address.

The phone dangles from my hand until the dial tone is replaced by a recorded voice asking me if I'd like to make a call. I jump and drop the receiver on the floor. Why didn't I say I'd go? It should have sounded like fun. But did Russ, with his friendly-smarmy voice, invite me up there on a pretext? Who knows what betrayal he has planned? I can't go. My legs won't let me. The back of my neck buzzes and I set my teeth against themselves.

I have to get some more crystal. There's no comfort in the house without it. Before I think any harder about leaving the safety of my apartment, I grab my coat and head out the door to the little club on the corner.

Hot Toddy is there, spinning records as guest celebrity DJ. Working as a DJ at Dance-o-Matic knights one with that lofty status, at least until a new club is crowned king. I stretch a smile across my teeth and bounce up to him, twirl a couple of times, and point up at the disco mirror ball. "That's so pretty. Like CRYSTAL," I shout.

Toddy nods and nonchalantly reaches for his canvas bag against the back wall.

I press a sweaty wad of bills into his palm. My palm is rewarded with two little packets. That simple. I just had to work up the nerve to leave the apartment. I put them in my pocket; the Joy Division song

Toddy plays spirals over me in my relief. I spin and see X-It, staring at me as if I'll turn into Fool's Gold at any moment.

Buoyed by my pocketful of promises, I sing along and direct every note, mindless of the lyrics' meaning, at X-It. I grasp his hands and dance. He looks over his shoulder to where Penny sits with the Mod Sisters. I grab his chin and redirect it toward me.

"X-It, I can be your best friend."

"You've always been my best friend, even these months you've been ignoring me."

Is that how he sees it? "Ignoring you?"

"Yeah, going to all those parties and not taking me."

"Is that what you want?"

He nods.

"I know you well enough to know I can now give you everything you want," I say. "I can make you shine brighter than gold." Voodoo's face, echoing similar words, flashes before me. I blink, and push him away.

"What do you mean?" X-It asks.

"I can get you into parties. Make you clever, outgoing. I can take away your fear." I narrow my eyes. "I can give you Andy Warhol. Tonight."

"Really? How? Do I have to leave Penny here?"

"Yes. Come to my place." My fingers play with the tiny plastic Baggies, sliding them against each other. "But you have to let me help you. You have to want me to. Do you want me to?"

"Well, yeah."

Doubt backwashes up my esophagus along with the bitter taste of speed that has post-nasal-dripped to my stomach. Can I do this? I'm not Voodoo, after all, and all my works are dull. I think of the intimacy involved as the needle will pierce X-It's skin and change his world. A thrill shoots through me.

I grab his hand to lead him home.

CHAPTER NINETEEN

X-It sits for me willingly on the closed toilet lid and offers his arm, I find his vein with no problem. I use works I washed in bleach. X-It doesn't voice any notice of the dull needle. He's so fit from his job, has such vascularity, that his veins bulge forth without the aid of a belt around his upper arm. With a flash of jealousy, I make a mental note to keep the excellent state of X-It's blood vessels from Voodoo's view. When or if he ever returns.

As the blood rush hits his throat, he coughs and slips off the toilet and into the bathtub in hysterical rapture. I copy him, landing next to him with the belt still around my arm. I sigh with relief, pleasure, and the feeling of never quite breathing in enough air after injecting crystal.

Cacophonous laughter echoes around the dry bathtub, punctuated by resounding bangs of feet and elbows. I roll against the cold porcelain, into X-It, and rest my head on him for a moment.

"You're right." X-It leans against the lip of the tub to smile at me. "This is really fun."

I tickle him. He pushes me away.

"Sor-ry," I say. He shrugs and I shove him back playfully. "Let's get up and go to Karisma's party."

He gives me a confused-puppy look.

"You didn't think we were going to stay in the tub all night?" I climb out and get to my feet.

"I was having fun."

"Come on. Warhol might be there."

He brightens but doesn't shift from the tub. "Only might?"

"I'll let you dress me," I tease.

He considers for a second. "In tinfoil?"

My gaze shoots skywards. At least it's summer and I won't be cold. I smile, nod, and extend my hand. "Tinfoil it is."

* * *

Andy Warhol resembles a small and frail ascetic from India, only much, much paler, and just as out of place on Karisma's black leather sofa. Assuming this is the real Andy Warhol. Rumor has it he sends fakes out into society. I elbow X-It in an attempt to get him to close his mouth.

With a, "So glad you could make it," and a barely perceptible double-take at my tin foil dress, Karisma grabs my other elbow and escorts me across the room, blaring introductions. This leaves X-It to continue to stand and stare.

"I brought you something," I say, lifting a Saks bag.

"A hostess gift?" inquires Karisma.

"Kinda." I hold the bag on its side and reach in, pulling out a tray with the panache of a fancy waiter.

"Ta da. Your head on a platter."

Karisma shrieks. And is silent. Then she approaches the object slowly, awe apparent on her regular features.

"You're giving this to me?" The cover girl is gone momentarily, replaced by a real girl. "You made this? I'm so beautiful. I never believed it. Photos lie you know." She reaches out an elegant finger to stroke the cheekbone of the decorated mannequin head. "I really am beautiful, aren't I?"

Without answer, I drift away from her.

Crikey is over by the shrimp cocktail, dipping and then dangling the little red crescents over his mouth before he pops them in. He remains down-to-earth, heedless of the impression he is making. I smile at the sight of him. Our eyes meet.

He holds out his hand to shake mine and ends up pointing at my dress. "This isn't a costume party, ya know, Missy," he says with a shrimp tail hanging out of his mouth. "You look like an ear of corn wrapped up. Care for a shrimp?"

"Oh!" I cry in pain as a cramp sears across my intestines. I clutch at my mid-section and unintentionally poke a couple of holes in the tin foil.

"No, thanks," I say softly. Damn Hot Toddy. Voodoo told me that speed that gives you cramps is cut with rat poison. This crystal definitely did not come from Voodoo's source.

Karisma appears at my elbow, and as if reading the direction of my thoughts. "Have you heard from the Gypsy? I do miss him."

"No. His business must be taking longer than he thought." I press my side and try not to grimace as another spasm strikes lightning in my gut.

"Young woman," says an icy quavering voice. I turn around. Andy Warhol points at me like the grim reaper and observes me intently from eyes I can hardly see behind his large eyeglasses and white bangs. He looks like a doll. Is this the real Andy Warhol?

"Young woman, your dress reminds me of my Factory." He lowers his hand. "The walls were silver. You should have seen it."

I wonder if I were there to see it, if I would have been potty trained at the time. I gather my wits.

"My dress was designed by this incredibly talented young man here." I indicate X-It. "May I introduce you?"

Introductions are made and soon X-It sits on the white shag carpet at Andy's feet like an expectant Greek student at the foot of Socrates.

He doesn't move all evening. Why isn't he suffering from cramps?

Crikey motions me back over to the shrimp. "I need to talk to you. One good turn deserves…you know."

"What are you talking about?"

"Come over here in the corner." After making sure we're alone he starts to talk about Voodoo.

I cut him off. "Did those scratches on your chest scar?"

He opens his shirt. "Camera doesn't pick it up. Karisma says you and Voodoo are living together, is that right?"

I make certain my tinfoil dress isn't splitting up the back. "Sort of. We're roommates." I feel very wrong and embarrassed about sleeping with him.

He rubs the intentional day-old stubble on his chin. "Well, Voodoo has always said you'd be his, always said that one day he'd own you. Made a point of it. I've never seen him more upset than when you left San Francisco. I never understood, seeing as how you never liked him much before, but now you're living together…"

"Crikey, what are you trying to say?"

"If Voodoo does come back, leaving him might be the right move. Just don't tell him I said so."

I shake away a chill. The feeling doesn't go with the décor in Karisma's apartment. Do I want Voodoo to return, really? I need him to come back, well supplied and with rent money, and I prefer to call him Marko, at least in my mind. Yes. I want him back.

But I say, "I don't think he's coming back." I lower my voice to a whisper, "But don't tell Karisma, okay?"

After Warhol leaves, X-It has no more stomach for the party and wants to leave too. I ask him if he has cramps because he certainly doesn't show it, and he answers only mild ones. He's so much stronger than I am.

"Let's go to our pier?" he asks.

I grin. He called it our pier. "Sure."

The cab driver is reluctant to leave us at the decaying dock, but accepts the fare and drives off. I take X-It's offered hand and step lightly onto the massive beams. Together, we hop over the dark sucking holes.

"I want to do some more." X-It grabs suddenly at my wrists. "Now. Come on. Let's do more."

Paranoia rushes me from all sides. Lapping black water looms. I'll lose him. I don't have any more.

"I can get some." I hurriedly tuck my hair behind my ears and feel the intense need to scratch my face. "Let's go to Sphinx. Toddy might still be there or we can find out what after party he went to."

X-It grins maniacally at me, a complete and total new convert. "I've got lots."

He pulls a handful of glistening mini-Baggies from his pants pocket. They slide on his palm.

"Careful!" I shout.

X-It returns the drugs to his pocket.

"How did you?" My eyes widen.

"A present." X-It's broad grin fills the night like a crescent moon.

"No way." My eyes get even wider.

X-It remains grinning, and silent.

I request a packet and then pour thin lines onto the back of his hand. We take turns snorting the magical powder.

"It's coke, not crystal," I say.

"So." He rolls his shoulders. "It's fun."

He wipes his hand on his shirt then slips it around my waist. With his other, he holds my hand and twirls me around the pier, avoiding the pitfalls.

I move closer to him as we dance. The giant Maxwell House Coffee sign glows at me from the opposite side of the river, and drips in time to our movement.

I lay my head on his shoulder. Our tempo slows.

Good to the last…

Drop. Drop. Drop.

X-It's mine. He's mine. He's mine.

CHAPTER TWENTY

Awake for five days straight now, I try to force my mind to rehearse an excuse for calling in sick again tomorrow. It's close to midnight. I stare blankly into the barren fireplace, counting and recounting each brick.

X-It is not satisfied with snorting lines. I have to administer more drugs into his bloodstream, and then more. Finally, my hand shakes too much to be able to hit his vein. I give up after causing him a hematoma. Voodoo's warnings resound like Tibetan gongs in my head.

The clink, clink of a spoon hitting the sides of a drinking glass comes from the kitchen. Because of my failure with the needle, X-It stirs white powder into a glass of lemonade.

Why won't he stop? Why can't he stop?

I want to come down with all the earnest anxiety of a kitten in a tree, and with the same inability to rescue myself. Desperately hunting sleep in the wrinkles of my thoughts, I seek the drink-of-cool-water satisfaction that unconsciousness will bring. My thirst is denied. My heart races. My skin crawls, sending caterpillars across my scalp. No more Quaaludes, no fresh works, and definitely no junk to make me go to sleep. But I know where to find some. I've watched the junkies go there since I moved here.

I have to get X-It to sleep, if only to stop him from doing any more coke. But he just drank some more. So to keep abreast, I mix a small amount in a spoon already encrusted with chemical remnants like a tiny Dead Sea. Maybe I can hit my own vein.

My jellyfish head swims atop my neck of tentacles. With difficulty focusing, I draw the liquid into the syringe and stick it into my arm, forgoing the use of alcohol, a belt, or even the proper angle of approach. Blood spreads, a ghastly purple spirit trapped underneath my skin. I pull out the needle, and with a mixture of pure scientific fascination and self-loathing, plunge it in again, deliberately missing the vein. More purple blossoms in the crook of my elbow and spreads outwards.

I plunge it in again.

And again.

I switch hands, poised to stab myself in my other arm.

"What're you doing?" X-It gives me a toddler grin.

"Getting ready to go get some junk."

He doesn't ask why the switch from speed to heroin, but cocks his head and asks, "Have you done it before?"

"No. Not yet."

I slide the hypodermic, capped but still full of coke and water, into a tin can beside the chaise. The can says Bugle Boy Tobacco on the side, and the syringe falls in among the others with the mundane clunk of a pencil returning to a pencil holder.

I say, "Crikey did it with Voodoo, and threw up all over the clean dishes in the dish drainer."

X-It looks disgusted, but he gets his jacket.

The first place we go to look is down on First Street, a place I've heard spoken of but wouldn't have gone if X-It hadn't been with me. Literally a hole in a wall, the place is called The Hole in the Wall. Damn. No candle flickers on the ledge of the hole. Just darkness. No one is there. I catch sight of police officers on the corner and sigh in frustration.

The cops push the drug trade from one block to another. The entire Lower East Side is riddled with dealers like a garden with gophers.

Plug up one hole and they appear at another. But what hole are they at tonight?

The cops eye me and X-It. They start toward us, swinging their clubs. I seize X-It's elbow and hasten back to Fifth Street.

"The shooting gallery will have some for sure," I whisper. "Maybe some fresh works too."

There is only one shooting gallery left now on Fifth Street between Avenues A and B.

I am about to enter the realm of my fantasies. Will junkies be lying on Persian carpets like in a painting of the lotus-eaters? Where do rock stars shoot up?

X-It puts his shoulder to the door. A dim stairwell rises up and up; a crack of light squints at us from the fourth floor landing. Smells of dank and rotting wood surround me. We follow the light upstairs.

The occupants behind the door on the fourth floor have been alerted by our incautious footsteps. Shuffling and mutterings in Spanish drift to my ears.

"*¿Que' usted desea?*"

I don't know the words, but the question is plain enough. "Junk. And works." I hold my breath. The door opens.

Dark eyes scan us up and down. "You poe-leece?"

X-It says, "We just wanna shoot up."

The door opens further. We take a few steps into the filthiest room I've ever seen.

"You shoot?" The man gestures to a cook pot on top of a glowing red hotplate that rests on a wooden crate turned on its side.

I stare in wretched horror. The light of the cook pot outlines others in the room. The scene is as far from lotus-eaters on Persian carpets as I can imagine. Portrayed in starkest chiaroscuro, the patrons of the shooting gallery are frozen in a twisted tableau version of Van Gogh's The Potato Eaters. One man stands, motionless, by the bubbling cook pot. His arm extends into space like a catatonic's. A hypodermic sticks into the back of his hand. A woman crouches on the floor. Others, of undetermined sex or feature, huddle in the corner.

"You shoot!" I am pushed toward the pot. Chest constricted, palms sweaty, I know if I use a needle in that room my life is over.

I step backwards. "Just want works. We shoot ourselves."

The man picks up a board. I spin to run from the room. The board connects with my shoulder blades and I stumble to the landing.

"Shit! The other guy's got a gun!" screams X-It.

We tear down the stairwell. I'm flying around the turns so fast I miss the opposite turn on the ground floor toward the door and freedom. X-It's wiry arm takes hold of mine and pulls me in the right direction.

Once out in the night air, he says, "Don't go home." He yanks me, hard, as I start to cross the street. "DON"T GO HOME. They're watching us."

"Fucking junkies," I exclaim as I rush to be under the safety of the streetlight. "Geez." I steady myself. "Okay fine, but we still need some junk. I know a friend of a friend of that girl, Fey Ray, whose band played at CBGB's last week."

"They were awful," he says with a backward glance as his steps quicken down the block, away from home.

"Fey Ray's friend lives off of St. Mark's. She's a go-go dancer."

"Huh." X-It replies, and rolls his shoulders.

After opening the door and letting us in, the friend of a friend wobbles in front of us, even though she has removed her high heels.

"Theese shooz," she speaks in a slurred eastern European accent and dangles the pumps. "Theese shooz are my lifeline."

She can't be more than seventeen or eighteen. Except she looks as well worn as her shoes.

"I am dancer. In Jer-zy."

X-It appears a bit frightened and disgusted at the girl's blowsy, stark sexuality.

"Do you know why we've come?" he asks.

She blinks. "For heroin. Fey says to tell poseurs who come knock we don't have any."

"Come on." X-It says to me, ignoring the girl. "Let's get some vodka and do laundry."

Later, I lean my head into X-It's shoulder with a sigh. It's four a.m. at the all-night laundromat. Cozy as warm lint, we sit on the table provided for folding clothes and watch the dryers go around. We pass the bottle back and forth.

At home with little stacks of clean clothes on my chaise lounge, I am a drunkie, which is way less chic than being a junkie, but there's still a chance I might puke on the dish drainer.

I lay my head on a pile of clothes. With a click, Voodoo's key turns in the lock.

CHAPTER TWENTY-ONE

New York City
Late July, 1981

Voodoo is distant and in his own world since his arrival. He barely takes notice of me and X-It. I sleep better, however, knowing my supplier is in the house. I should feel guilty that he came back and put himself in danger. If I told him that, he'd only laugh and tell me it was his business.

It's Saturday, and I only have a short shift at the bakery. On my way out the door to work, I pass X-It's unused messenger's bike parked in the hallway and give the seat and handlebars a bittersweet caress. My route will take me past the health food grocery where he now works.

X-It is mine. Sort of. He divides his time between his official, rent-paid home at Penny's and the pillows under the palm trees in my living room. I only spend the night with Voodoo when X-It sleeps at Penny's. Voodoo has picked up on this, but hasn't said anything.

At the health food store, I pretend to peer inside the ears of organic white sweet corn arranged in the sidewalk bin beneath the green canvas awning. X-It comes out in his matching green canvas apron, smiling.

"Those are from upstate," he says, and touches one lovingly. "Too expensive. And they'll probably rot because everyone who can afford to buy them is either in the Hamptons or at Fire Island. God it's hot."

"Is it cooler inside?"

"Over by the refrigerated produce."

I follow him. He picks up a spray mister attached to a coiled hose and gives the greens a bath so it looks like he's working while we talk.

"Do you miss it?" I ask.

"Miss what? Not eating organic? No way. Everything that goes into your body should be pure."

I choke back my astonishment. "No, I mean being a messenger."

X-It looks at the ground and water sprays the wall. "Sure. I guess. It just got too hard."

He moves over to fluff the bean sprouts and continues in a slightly defensive tone, "This isn't bad you know. Only the kind of people who can get into the fourth floor of Dance-o-Matic can work produce. It's not like we're cashiers or anything."

He holds a bean sprout close to his face as he prepares to bite it. I notice no difference between his complexion and the waxy yellow of the sprout, as if both he and the bean seed live underground. He should ride his bike for fun to get some fresh air. But he won't.

I don't think he's done any drugs since our chaste honeymoon-esque binge. X-It will not go out to a club, a party, a restaurant, a film festival, a museum, or a laundromat without me. He craves my new connections. But being well-known and well-liked is not the same as being famous. I am not famous. And X-It does not sleep with me.

I turn to go.

"J.J."

I spin back.

"Catch." He tosses a nutrition bar at me. "You're too thin."

Impossible. But I'll eat it anyway.

"J.J." He stops me again. "I want to move back."

I beam my brightest Holly Golightly smile at him. "Really?"

He nods.

"Cool. We can go get your stuff the next day off we have together. Next week, right?"

He crunches another bean sprout; his hand shakes a little. "I think so."

My victory is nearly complete. Next week all will be as it was.

As I walk down St. Mark's Place, the rumbling of four motorcycles coming up behind sends me skittering into a vintage clothing store. I peer through the fringe of a blue leather vest. The salesgirl pops gum and stares at me like she's taking notes for a novel. When the bikers have safely passed, I continue my walk to work.

Later that afternoon at the bakery, I reach deep into the pastry case with a sanitary waxed tissue to get the specific apple turnover requested by the customer, a sour faced old man. The sleeve of my Fifties polka dot blouse catches on the shelf above and stretches back.

"Junkie!" the man screams, spilling his hot coffee on his arm and down the glass case. He screams some more. "Dirty junkie! Don't touch my food. I'm not eating here."

He tosses his coffee cup in the trash, splashing brown liquid down the wall.

Eileen, the assistant baker, bustles in, looking surprised and plump and wholesome in her checked baker's pants, white coat, puffy hat, and flour-dusted cheeks. Her mouth opens.

Two young men on their way home from Wall Street, in need of brownies, stare at me and my beautiful midnight blue hair as if they just scraped me from their shoes.

"Fucking junkies," says one to the other on their way out the door.

Eileen steps over to me as I rise from my kneeling position behind the pastry case, seizes my wrist, and turns it over. Track marks, old and new, dot the insides of my slender, youthful arms. The deep bruises and trapped pools of blood from the night I repeatedly jabbed myself are faded to yellow but still evident. My arms look as if they're something forgotten in the back of the fridge.

I see myself through Eileen's eyes. A stupid girl who betrayed the trust placed in her. A disgusting girl.

"You're fired."

"I'm not a junkie."

"You're fired."

I take off my white apron, place it on the counter, pull down my sleeves, and leave.

I sit out on my and X-It's rotting pier until nightfall—eating the nutrition bar for dinner—until the Maxwell House coffee cup perks on. Then I walk home through Greenwich Village and avoid making eye contact with anyone. Each footstep beats out a self-flagellating mantra that carries me to Avenue A in a zombie fog.

Junkie.

Glamour. Junkie.

Fame. Junkie. Weak.

Junkie. Illusion. Junkie.

Vomit. Junkie. Rage. Junkie. Punk. Junkie.

"I'm not a junkie," I tell myself as I shrug my shoulders and stretch my neck. "But, geez, I need some speed."

As I approach the dark door to Sphinx, I see it's open. Has the earth shifted on its axis? It's never open. Dirt and debris shoot out the doorway in rhythmic spurts. Someone is sweeping up before opening time. Looking past Sphinx to Fifth Street, I think I see Voodoo outside our apartment building. Yes, there he is, with two other men. The two bikers move in on him in a menacing way.

I have to do something. I raise my hand to wave and begin to call out, "Voo—"

Air whooshes out of me as an arm connects around my diaphragm in an orangutan swoop and drags me into club Sphinx.

"Shhh."

Stale beer, cigarette, and Lysol odors swamp me in the darkness. From the smell, I could be in any bar in the United States.

I squirm. "What the he—?"

"Shhh. It's me. Todd," the DJ whispers. He holds me back from the doorway. "You don't want those guys to know you're connected with the Gypsy."

"But they'll hurt him!"

"Too late. Now whisper."

I hiss, "What's going on?"

"Remember that stuff I sold you?"

"The rat poison?" I glare at him as my eyes adjust to the darkness.

"Well those biker guys sell that stuff in this town. In most every town. They make it. You've seen their headquarters down on Third Street, right?" He eases up on his grip and motions me to a barstool. I start to peer out the door and he shakes his head. "Don't look."

Poor Marko. "I've got to go to him."

"Wait 'til those guys are gone." He opens a beer and slides it to me. "Let me explain it to you this way. Now, if you were part of a large business organization that controlled manufacture and distribution of a product, would you appreciate someone else coming in, a lone wolf, with connections to large amounts of a higher quality product?"

"But that's capitalism." I start to put two and two together about Voodoo's extended business trip.

"This is organized crime. Different laws."

I take a sip and remember I now have only one job. Hopefully the beer is free. "So you know these guys?"

"I'm a small time dealer who works in trendy nightclubs." He manages to swing his hair off his shoulder in a self-deprecating gesture. "To them I'm a middleman. A customer." He meets my eyes across the bar. "Hey, wee lassie from Frisco," he warns. "Don't let them see you."

I don't tell him his warning is too late.

A half hour later, I scan the streets and then make a dash for my apartment building. Voodoo is not on the sidewalk and neither is any sign of spattered blood.

I let myself in.

He lounges nonchalantly under the palm trees, untouched and as darkly virulent as ever.

"You're okay!"

He smiles, showing white wolf-teeth, pleased with my show of concern. "Why wouldn't I be? You look a bit rattled though."

"Yeah. Edgy. I could sure use some … " I reach in my purse for my speed compact when I remember those threatening bikers. "Uh, do you have any H?" *Junkie. Junkie.*

"What?" His head snaps up.

"I just got fired for being a junkie. I may as well celebrate and actually try heroin." I've slowed my drug use down since Voodoo's return. I only shoot up when I think I'll jump in front of a subway train if I don't.

"I have the purest brown I brought back with me from California. It's even better than China White. Not for you, though."

"Please?" He knows I won't go across the street to the shooting gallery, and Fey Ray and her underage Hungarian stripper were busted two weeks ago.

"You're a wisp of a thing." The side of his mouth angles down as he deliberates. "It would be so easy to make you fade away."

I startle at his last words, then realize by his smile he's joking.

"Here's half a 'lude." He holds out the pill. "But only if you have sex with me here beneath the palms."

"A whole 'lude," I say and he grins.

Afterward, we lay curled up together on the pillows like two napping cats. He strokes my hair as we watch replays of the royal wedding of Charles and Diana on his small portable television. Diana's steps seem too slow, as if her dress weighs her down, or she is ascending to the guillotine instead of walking down the aisle. It must be the Quaalude, too strong. I fight off the fog of unconsciousness.

Diana is the same age as Karisma, not too much older than me. Laughing under my breath, I imagine myself, punk hair and army boots, marrying the Prince of Wales in St. Paul's Cathedral. My dark prince continues to pet my hair. I try to gather my thoughts and turn my attention to his biker problem.

"How did you s-s-stop those men fwom hurting you?" My words slur through the mist.

He stops stroking my hair. "You saw?"

"I hid. At Shwinx." On speed I'm Holly Golightly. On 'ludes I'm Elmer Fudd.

"Good." He pulls his pentacle from his pocket and twirls it. "I know how to protect myself."

"Bikers aren't scared of that Satanic bullshwit. They pwactically invented it."

"No." He rises up on one elbow and meets my eyes in a steady stare. "There's more to it than that, as you know."

"Weawy, how did wu get wid of da bikers?"

He ignores me and says, "I find your strength intriguing, a challenge."

Strength? What's he saying? I'm a weak person. I wish my mind could think.

"I forgive you for engineering Crikey's departure from our group," he says with a smile and rubs his hand between my shoulder blades. "It made it all the more satisfying when I won, and got you in return."

The words "won" and "got you" make it through my haze, the rest sounds crazy. "Huh? What are you talking about, Marko?"

He continues in that spooky vein, "And X-It must give up something if I'm to share you with him."

"Wha?" I protest. "But we're not—"

"Shhh."

I hear X-It coming through the entryway. I lower my voice and speak in a rush, "You should gewout of town for a bit. Those biker guys are bad news."

Voodoo throws back his head—his necklace of teeth claws at his throat—and roars with laughter.

"What's so funny?" asks X-It, coming through the door with a paper sack of groceries.

"I was laughing at your secret," says Voodoo.

Through lids that threaten to close, I observe X-It. He doesn't ask what secret. His face turns ashen and he silently veers to the kitchen to put away the food.

"Your secret's out, buddy." Voodoo shakes the baggie of brown.

X-It appears to relax a little. When the food is in the refrigerator he joins us on the pillows and rolls up his sleeve.

So many track marks.

I regard him quizzically. "X-It, do you even like junk?"

He looks smug, of all things. "I could do it everyday."

Voodoo laughs. "Could and do."

"What?" I try to push up on my arms but they won't work, so I just lie on the pillow. A small amount of drool I can't stop wets the fabric and my cheek.

"Yeah." X-It is joyful, a partial weight off his shoulders. He says in a teasing tone, "You're a poser, J.J." He smirks. "I'm a real junkie."

I look from X-It to Voodoo and back again. Every cell in my numb body rebels at the thought of X-It, beautiful, talented X-It, as one of the damned catatonic "Potato Eaters" across the street. The angry, judgmental face of the old man in the bakery rises up and screams at me. *Dirty junkie!*

Voodoo laughs again, his creep show laugh. I attempt to stand and end up hurling my body off the pillows like a semi-paralyzed snake. I crawl on my belly. When the cold tile sears the skin on my stomach, I know I'm in the bathroom. I curl up and kick the door shut. Dark enfolds me, save the crack of light from beneath the door.

My fault. All my fault.

X-It taps. He says in his plaintive voice, "I thought you'd be jealous 'cause I did it first." He sighs. "J.J., that's why I didn't tell you. Don't be angry with me. Voodoo asked me not to tell. He told me you'd admire me as a junkie. He said you worshiped junkies. J.J., come on."

His dependency on heroin will ruin everything I do admire and worship about him. Apparently it has already taken his job as a bicycle messenger, taken his strength and vigor. And with time it will take away his drive to do anything with his talent. And it might take away his life.

Sick all over, gagged by guilt, I want a whole syringe-full of brown heroin. "So easy to make her fade away." I mutely beg to be kicked over the cliff, to tumble into total eternal blackness.

CHAPTER TWENTY-TWO

New York City
August, 1981

I am not a junkie, but I may as well be. Each day drags on. Each night I dream of bikers, broken arms, and X-It's vacant eyes. Every time I hear a motorcycle outside my window I come close to shitting my pants. It's a glamorous New York life.

X-It floats into my room wearing loose pants and a tunic. The weightless quality to his walk is new, but he shrugs his shoulders like the same old X-It.

"What's with the hippy threads?" I ask him as I stretch out my feet in my army boots.

"They're pure Egyptian cotton. They breathe."

I've noticed his shallow inhalation pattern since he gave up being a messenger, and I'm glad his clothes are breathing for him. The open-toe sandals do their part as well.

"You look like hell," he says with his usual frankness.

He's right. I look ill. The ups and downs of speed and 'ludes confuse my body's rhythms, turn them into an avant garde composition, all screeching lack of melody, and if a backbeat exists, it's hard to feel.

I must find some good concealer. X-It won't stay with me if I'm hideous.

"Okay," I ask him. "So are we going over to Penny's to pick up the rest of your stuff?"

Voodoo is out, which is good. Since I only spend the night with him when X-It isn't here, he's not too pleased about X-It moving back full time. But he doesn't seem horribly put out, at least to my face. He even looks amused, sometimes, as if he's a film director watching dailies of scenes he shot.

"Alright, we'll go," says X-It companionably. "I just need to get a drink of water first."

As he leaves to go to the kitchen, I picture him pouring distilled, pure-H2O from a plastic jug into a glass.

I mumble in his direction, "I've ruined your life. Just so I can be near you."

"What did you say? I'm ready."

"Nothing. Let's go."

We walk across town to Penny's SoHo apartment. X-It shuffles along in his sandals like he's eighty. My mind skips along by itself, while my body is reduced to the drudgery of keeping my heart beating and lungs pumping. Sweat rolls down the insides of my arms. By the time we reach her building I'm fighting off swirling black clouds at the edges of my vision. I can't faint now, my moment of triumph is here.

X-It finds the key in his pocket and lets us in.

He climbs the stairs to his room to retrieve his stuff. He's almost completely mine.

"Penny's not here," he says, dropping a pillow over the balcony railing. "She asked her parents to send her to fashion school in London."

"What?" I grab the exposed brick wall.

"Yeah. She took off. I'm glad she's not here." He speaks more loudly as he disappears, "I wouldn't want to see her sad that I'm leaving."

He didn't show me the same consideration when he moved out.

So he only wanted to move back with me because Penny left? My nose twitches. "Are you in love with Penny?"

How did that slip out? But now that it has, I want an answer.

X-It comes back out and stares at me as if I sprouted antennae. "Penny's my friend."

Oversized black and white acrylic paintings lean against the brick walls and iron banisters. Not bad, but derivative. Still, they're better than I thought Penny could pull off. I think of art school. The vision of coffee spreading over the receptionist's desk and papers turns into coffee running down the glass case in the bakery.

Dirty junkie. Go ahead, join X-It. I might as well be a junkie. It's not as if I'll be sacrificing any talent. I don't have any.

"I'll be just a minute," X-It disappears again.

Something odd, and bad, catches my attention.

"X-It," I call out. "Does Penny have any mannequins?"

As I say it, a queasy sensation erupts in my stomach, accompanied by small stabbing pains in my intestines, the arches of my feet contract, more sweat breaks out on my skin.

"Why would she have any mannequins? That would be your territory."

Ah, so he isn't completely unobservant. I put a hand to my stomach and look over my shoulder, uneasy.

"X—"

He appears at the railing and swings his duffle bag over. It lands at my feet with a thud.

"Get down here," I say with urgency.

He uses the stairs.

"Are you sure she doesn't have any mannequins?" It would be so like Penny to pull a sick joke on me.

"You're all freaked out," X-It rolls his shoulders. "You've got to stop with that speed shit."

I point. "There's a blue foot sticking out behind the couch."

X-It is so close behind me I can smell his Dr. Bonner's castile soap. I creep over to the foot.

Between the back of the retro-kitsch couch and the floor-to-ceiling loft windows, lies Pyro. Her lifeless body is dressed in a tee shirt and panties.

We kneel on either side of her. There's something in an envelope beside her—pure California brown heroin—and a hypodermic beside its torn wrapper. A lit candle is on a side table. Consciousness thins, and the room spins. I make retching noises.

"Not here," X-It cautions. "Don't leave signs we've been here."

I make it to the toilet, flush, and lean against the wall. It's a little better now I can't see what's left of Pyro. X-It peers into the bathroom.

I say, "We have to call the police."

"Uh-uh. No way. We both have enough track marks to send us straight to Riker's Island." X-It shrugs.

Footsteps and the stirrings of people waking up come from upstairs. I look at him, the question plain in my eyes.

He rolls his shoulders and shrugs again. "I don't know who's here. I only went in my room," he says softly. "It's probably the Mod Sisters or Dogbite."

I am a coward. I don't want to be here when Dogbite discovers his dead sister. I tug the cotton sleeve of X-It's tunic. He fetches his duffle and silently, together, we slip through the kitchen and out the back door into the alley.

As I reach the street my strides lengthen until I'm almost running. Pure paranoid panic takes over. Connections will be made. The police will come to my apartment. I run flat out. X-It, hampered by flapping clothes, flat sandals and drugs, can't keep up and is left behind. My fingers dig rabidly through my purse as my feet fly through SoHo. My fingers close around my beloved speed compact. I halt at a corner trashcan, open the latch, and dump out every particle of powder. The compact lands deep inside. My lungs burn.

I have to get home. Fast. Faster. I must get rid of the works—sitting out in the open—in the tobacco can by my chaise lounge. If only I could scrub off my track marks. I run through SoHo and over into the Lower East Side. Each breath scorches my lungs. This can't be my body. My body sprints like a greyhound. Did. Before.

The vroom of a motorcycle scares me. I jump back, and see the same biker who threatened me roar past. He has something long, wrapped in cloth, on his back. He turns toward the East Village.

My mind can only think, *no no, no, no.*

I push my leaden legs until they ache. My brain can't get enough oxygen. It takes an age to travel two blocks. And two more blocks. I am filled with terror, but just like in my nightmares, my feet don't respond and the sidewalk pulls at them.

By the time I get close to home, anything could have happened. Everything looks fuzzy, hazy even, as I turn onto Avenue A. Acrid air stings my nostrils.

Smoke.

I increase my speed as much as I can, because without even looking I know my apartment is on fire. A taxi pulls up and X-It jumps out. Sensing my urgency, he rushes through the entry doors and unlocks the apartment.

Too late I caution, "Check if it's hot."

He shoves open the door. Smoke rolls out but no flames. He stands and stares in fascination. I push him toward his room.

"Your portfolio. Get it."

"It's not that important." He blinks in the smoke.

"GET IT!"

I unlock the deadbolt to my room and gaze around. None of my artwork is worth saving. Oddly, the only thing I want is the videotape Russ gave me of the night my paintings were shredded. Tucking the tape under my arm, I debate throwing away the can of works in case the fire isn't thorough. I snatch it up and throw it out the hall window into the vacant lot next door.

X-It trots up to me, coughing, portfolio in hand and that damn Warhol picture with it. "Voodoo's not here. Let's go."

Something makes me poke my head into the bathroom.

I shriek. Horror, awful and shattering, makes me feel like I fly up and out of my body to hover near the ceiling. Looking down through what seems a long tunnel, I try to make sense of what is left of Voodoo, of Marko.

His arms hug the base of the toilet, wrists handcuffed together behind it. Black heeled boots extend toward me. Black jeans travel up to a red denim shirt with mother of pearl buttons. Just as the mother of pearl buttons float on the red of his shirt, bits of white porcelain, white tiger's teeth, and Voodoo's own teeth and bone, swim in a red viscous sea. Blood-soaked tendrils of hair, like seaweed, cling to pieces of what once was his head.

X-It's grip on my wrist sucks me back into my body. He pulls me from the bathroom and out of the apartment. Flames lick around the doorway as we emerge into the street. A crowd gathers. Even some of the potato eaters are braving daylight.

Sirens blare, louder, closer. The windows into the basement apartment are broken and that level of the building is completely engulfed in flames. The man who hit me across the back with a board now meets my gaze as if we're brother and sister.

"A man, with shotgun, threw fireball in there." He points first at the basement window and then up at the boarded and broken window of the fourth floor shooting gallery, to indicate from where he'd seen it. Such a witness to such a death.

Hot Toddy comes running over from Sphinx. He slips his arm around my shoulders. X-It lets him.

"You look pretty shook up," he says. "My place is close."

I throw his arm off of me and turn on him, teeth bared. Words will not form in my mouth.

Hot Toddy backs away, hands raised. The sirens grow deafening. Fire trucks careen around the corner. X-It seeks eye contact.

He says, "We need to get lost."

In agreement, I turn to flee with him. But he vanishes, alone, into the gathered crowd.

CHAPTER TWENTY-THREE

In the women's shower at the YMCA on 34th Street, I scrub at my skin until it turns an indignant red. No matter how much soap I use, I can't get the smell of smoke out of my flesh. Like a water glass leaves behind a ring, the image of Voodoo's corpse leaves an indelible mark on my brain. Every time I close my eyes it's there.

I slather on gardenia-scented shampoo I picked up at the drugstore, not caring if my hair color fades as a result. I deserve to be dead. Does Marko? Doesn't matter now. I think I might have loved him. It's stupid and paranoid, but an overwhelming fear that police or bikers will storm the YMCA at any moment makes me shiver despite the hot water. Did I really throw away my drugs?

Where is X-It, anyway? Marko is gone and I have lost X-It.

The YMCA seems like the best place for me. Having to deal with Toddy or Russ is out of the question, and Pyro's overdose makes connection with the other asteroids imprudent. Karisma? I don't kid myself. My new friends are people you invite to parties, not disasters. Crikey will help me, but shame makes me shy away from that option.

Perfume of gardenia fights with the smoke in my hair and wins. I will despise the smell of gardenias from this day forward. I squeeze shampoo into my palm and wash my skin. The shower water, just short of scalding, beats down upon me. It taps and spatters on the curtain, opaque with soap scum; it gurgles as it swirls clockwise around the large floor drain.

Under the blistering water and steam my head swims and pulses. Dizzy, I glance around the tiled room. Naked vulnerability makes me shake. I panic, remembering my first night in this place. I close my eyes.

Leave. I must leave New York. Or die here.

Jolted, my lids fly open. The shower room is filled with steam and nothing more.

Later, clean and damp, I perch on the narrow bed in the monkish Y room. Not too unlike a room in a mental hospital, I imagine.

The level of chemicals I've become habituated to are rapidly dropping to nothing in my bloodstream. My jaws clamp of their own accord. My calves spasm. What idiot said crystal meth isn't physically addictive? Getting high right now would help, but I'm too afraid to leave my room.

In the morning, I dress in my smoky, torn lace flapper dress and boots. They're the only clothes I now own. When the bank opens I withdraw all of my money, five hundred and twenty-eight dollars, and go for coffee and a doughnut at the Chock Full of Nuts. As I stir my coffee, I imagine myself as the woman at the diner counter in that ghostly Hopper painting. Only this is broad daylight, and a menacing leather-jacketed biker sits across from me.

I must leave New York or die.

I down my coffee, grab my doughnut and flee. I'm a witness. Will the motorcycle gang target me next? I touch the track marks on the inside of my elbow like a rosary. My stomach lurches. I'll end up like Pyro, or worse.

But, how can I leave X-It?

Queasy after passing the smells of a steamed hot dog vendor, I clutch at my stomach and toss the remaining doughnut in the trash. Now near Macy's, I see the mannequins in the windows and scan them, looking for my work. In the August heat, the window display depicts fall leaves, and pom-pom and pennant waving sorority girls off to college.

A hollow emotion scoops out my insides and fills them with anxiety and loss. I missed that train to normalcy, it left the station without me. I pull up short. X-It left me.

Galvanized, I push my way into the department store. After braving the hauteur of the underpaid salesgirls, I buy the most flowery dress I can find, along with shoes, and change in the store. I leave the smoky, torn lace dress and army boots on the floor of the dressing room.

Back at the YMCA, I wait in line at the single ancient payphone and try not to eavesdrop. When it's my turn, the mouthpiece smells like beef and onion perogi. I wipe it with my sleeve and then call my supervisor at the mannequin factory to tell her I'm quitting and not coming back.

As I prepare to make my second phone call—the man waiting behind me makes harrumpfing sounds—I realize I should have reversed the order of my calls. What if Michael says no?

The phone rings and picks up.

"Hello Michael? This is J.J."

"Uh." An awkward pause follows. "This is Art. Remember me?"

So long ago. "Sure, Art. Is Michael there?"

"No."

Damn. "Tell him…" Tiresome tears start. "Tell him I'm coming. Today."

I hang up and hail a taxi.

"Take me to JFK airport," I say. "Wait." I watch the back of the driver's head. "First stop on Fifth Street between Avenues A and B."

The driver's black bristle haircut, ending under the collar of a military jacket, doesn't invite further conversation. His hands rub the steering wheel compulsively before each turn. I look away.

Viewing the changing Manhattan neighborhoods from the boundaries of the cab's passenger window gives me a bit of objectivity, not unlike the way a film director frames a scene with his hands. I no longer view the streets, stores, and stoplights as an inhabitant. I'm leaving.

Where will I eat dinner tonight? Will I sleep at Michael's? Or at the airport? I sigh, coming close to a state of overwhelmed catatonia.

"Are you sure you want to stop here?" The cabbie says as he pulls in front of the charred apartment building. It now matches the others on the opposite side of the street. A half laugh, half snort escapes me as I wonder how long it will take for a shooting gallery to spring up here.

"Yes, please," I answer him. "I lived here yesterday."

A flicker of interest registers as the cabdriver assesses me in the rearview mirror.

"Oh." He puts the car in Park. "Meter's running."

"Fine. Please wait."

Small ghosts of smoke still escape here and there, and the blackened remains give off warmth. Gentle alarm bells sound somewhere between my ears, but I ignore them and push past the yellow caution tape. The entire side of the building that borders the vacant lot no longer exists.

I edge around the remaining foundation wall, which extends down into the black-hole basement apartment. I hold a sooty beam for support and wipe my hair out of my face. I vow not to touch my new dress. Leave it to me to buy new clothes and still end up on Michael's doorstep looking like Oliver Twist.

I survey the destruction. Most of what was my and X-It's apartment doesn't exist anymore. The bitter stench is overpowering. I'll have to use my gardenia shampoo again. Maybe even at the airport.

Moving closer, my mouth falls open. Charred mannequin arms reach up from the cellar like victims begging to be saved. Their graceful, stylized gestures make their doomed petition all the more poignant.

I paw the air in front of me in an effort not to fall off of the wall and into the pit of black ash and torn pipes.

"Wow," says the cabdriver, who exited the taxi without my being aware of it. He grabs my elbow and pulls me off the wall. "That's some bad juju." He shakes his head at the ruin.

I burst into tears. He looks at me as if I'm insane.

"Are you going to the airport or not?"

I nod, knowing my tears must be rivulets through the soot on my face. After returning to the cab, he shuts the car door with me inside. The taxi pulls away. Glad the driver faces forward, I let the tears come.

JuJu was my father's pet name for me. That's some bad JuJu. The words echo around my head accompanied by the uninvited image of my father's face leering at me in his swimming pool.

Glancing over at the burnt building and fallen timbers, I see instead the twisted and charred wreckage of a twin engine Piper Cub. My mother had me take the newspaper article and photo of his airplane accident to school for show and tell.

I'm going to San Francisco. San Francisco isn't far from "me and Martin in Moss Beach…" I might visit my mother. I might not.

I pay the cabbie after he pulls to the airline's curb. I ignore his quizzical look at my lack of luggage. All I have is my purse, which is all he should be concerned about. I pay him. Inside, I go from airline counter to airline counter looking for an available seat on a flight to San Francisco today.

Eventually I book three connecting flights with stopovers in Chicago and Denver. I won't arrive until very late tonight, California time. I settle into the chair at the gate to wait for boarding. I can't believe I'm truly leaving New York. Leaving X-It.

CHAPTER TWENTY-FOUR

I tap my knees on the underside of my tray table in the cramped space allotted on the jetliner, earning disapproving glances from the businessman in the next seat. The underside of my fingernail against my bottom teeth tastes like soap from the Dallas airport ladies room. I'm on the last leg of my journey, approaching San Francisco International Airport. My neck pops as I stretch it to one side. The businessman raises his gaze from his paperwork and glares again.

Gawd, but coffee is a poor substitute for speed. After about twelve cups and as many trips to the bathroom climbing over the businessman's knees, I want to scream. Somebody. SOMEBODY, must have some speed on this airplane. Hell, Mr. Businessman probably has some coke in his suit pocket. I grit my teeth, snarl like a tiger, and rub my forehead hard.

Sick of fluorescent lights with their blinking and humming—in the terminals, in the bathrooms, on the planes—I shut my eyes. A migraine threatens. I sigh, hoping for an end to this interminable day in and out of airbuses and airports, being chased back across the country by the image of Voodoo's splattered corpse.

I don't really want speed, I remind myself. I'm just used to using it.

Yes, I do. I want it. As I run my hand over the inside of my arm in anticipation of getting high, I straighten my legs under the seat in front of me and issue a moan that borders on sexual. I open my eyes, bring my knees up abruptly and smash the tray table. I grab my coffee just in time. The businessman heaves a sigh.

The antimacassar on the seat in front of me slips as I straighten it from behind. The woman sitting in that seat turns around to look and catches the eye of the businessman. He cocks his head to me, as if my colored hair and absurd flowered dress are the reasons for my behavior. The woman nods and turns back around.

Can I tear the tray table from its hinges and bash both of them over the head? I take another sip of black coffee and force myself to be still. My eyelid twitches. I should have grabbed a wig off a mannequin when I bought this sham outfit at Macy's. Perhaps my hair does mark me as a screw up, just as Voodoo used his upside down pentacle to mark him as…as what? Marko. When I think of him as Marko, I'm so regretful I can't wrap my feelings around what happened.

I feel even sorrier for Michael. Even though I have no suitcases, I'll be getting off that plane with a tremendous load of baggage. No man can carry it. I laugh out loud, and hear a ding. But Michael won't be there waiting for me. He's no fool.

"May I help you sir?" The flight attendant arrives to answer the businessman's summons, and then reaches up to turn off his call button. In answer he simply points at me.

The stewardess smiles. "I see." She switches her attention to me, and now is not smiling. "Excuse me, miss, would you mind following me?"

"I'm taking my coffee." I grasp the cup.

"That's fine. I'll bring you some more. Now, please follow me."

I both hate and envy the woman's mincing walk and assuredness in heels while in mid-air, but I follow those pantyhose-encased legs to the back of the plane near the bathroom. There, are two empty seats. The flight attendant points. I sit, and promptly open both tray tables.

Fresh hot coffee arrives, poured from a gleaming silver pot, and I flip through a magazine. Karisma this. Karisma that. The girl is so hot they coined a new term, supermodel.

Super dirty junkie, I want to scream. I tear at the page. The stewardess arrives. "May I have that back, miss?"

"I'll stop. I'll treat it nice." I assure the polite, mannequin-like flight attendant. The woman nods and returns to the galley. But three pages later, I burst into tears. A model with a ginger pageboy reminds me of Penny.

London? I'd better find X-It before he follows her. Damn, I'm flying six hundred miles an hour in the wrong direction.

I take a sip of scalding coffee and burn my tongue. I deserve it. Will Michael let me stay at his house? I'm an awful person, should I allow him to?

I can't wrap my mind around so much, so I tear apart a napkin instead, leaving it on the seat next to me. Unconsciousness beckons like a faraway oasis.

Pulling twelve wadded dollars out of my pocket, I hold them out to the passing flight attendant and ask, "How much vodka can I get for this?"

The woman stops, tray in hand. "None. Unless you have proper I.D. But I'll bring you a Fresca in a moment."

Shit, legal drinking age in New York is eighteen, but not in the sky. I move the window shade up and down, up and down, waiting. Just as I decide more coffee is the ticket, the stewardess arrives with two plastic cups of clear beverage. The Fresca must be flat, no bubbles. I take a sip. Pure Vodka. The flight attendant winks at me and sashays up the aisle, collecting trash. I down both glasses, cough, and slump back across both seats, anesthetized. Either the stewardess is a sympathetic cokehead, or she sent the berserk zoo animal a tranquilizer dart.

* * *

The terminal appears as if in a dream. I struggle along the moving walkway, trying to stay upright. At twelve-thirty in the morning, only a few red-eye travelers and the security night shift move about. More flashing fluorescent lights, everywhere I look, confuse me, but I locate the escalator down to the baggage carousels. Halfway down I remember I have no baggage to claim. Looking out the glass doors, I see a few taxis waiting for late night passengers. But where will I go?

I decide to sleep the night in the terminal, and in the morning I'll take a bus to Moss Beach and find my mom. Scanning the uncomfortable looking seats near the windows, I think I'll go back upstairs and find an out-of-the-way gate to crash at. I turn the corner and trip over the feet of a man sleeping near baggage carousel number four.

"Excuse me," I mutter.

"Er, yup," says the man sleepily.

"Michael?"

Overwhelmed by the fact he showed up, and disappointed by his lack of good sense, I say, "You're here."

I shift from foot to foot, wary as a feral cat, waiting for him to chase me off. He takes off his Buddy Holly glasses, rubs his eyes, and then massages his shoulder.

"Art told me you were coming today." He replaces his glasses and looks at his watch. "Technically, it's tomorrow."

Irritated at being so far in his debt within seconds of meeting, I say, "You could have waited for me to show up at your door."

"Uh, he said you didn't sound good at all. Besides, we changed apartments from where we lived before, when you and Art were, uh, dating. Look," he says crisply, "I told you to call me if you needed to and you did. No big deal. Car's out there. Where are your bags?"

Imagining the ton of invisible baggage chained to me, I burst out in hysterical laughter. He stares at me, mouth open. It's his turn to be on his guard. At his look, I stop abruptly and muffle a cough.

"Just this." I pat my purse, look down at the carpet, and then sneak my gaze back to him.

His straight eyebrows are topped with slicked back hair. He manages to appear nerdy and hip at the same time in an old windbreaker, black jeans, and high top tennies.

"You mean you don't have a toothbrush or anything to sleep in?

"Nope."

Fatigue and annoyance evident in his voice, he asks, "Are you making fun of me? I know I say 'Yup.'"

"No. I'm not." I shift the strap of my purse on my shoulder. "I don't have anything because everything in my apartment burned down yesterday. Including Voodoo, who was shot in the head. And Pyro OD'd. And…and X-It disappeared."

During the long pause that follows, the only sounds are the hum of the fluorescent lights and the well-oiled click, click of the escalators.

"Shit," he says. "Come on. You can wear one of my tee shirts and sleep on the couch."

CHAPTER TWENTY-FIVE

San Francisco
September, 1981

The couch and jammies arrangement has been working okay for two weeks. Michael is friendly but wary. I am on the best behavior I can manage, but it will never be good enough. I try not to think about what my next steps will be.

Michael prepares artichokes and garlic bread for dinner. Art and I sit at the dining table and wait for his feast to appear. I don't know what to say to Art. He ducks and dodges me as much as he can.

"Do you like artichokes?" I venture to ask him.

He shifts his gaze from the bookshelf to the window and its café curtains, anywhere but at my face. "Uh, sure. Who doesn't?"

"I've never had one," I say.

Michael pops up at the doorway, garlic press in hand, and a too-big smile on his face. "What kind of Californian are you?"

I smile weakly back at him. He's been so nice to me these past two weeks.

"You're really going to enjoy dinner tonight, then. But you can't have artichokes without this." With a grand flourish he places a jar of mayonnaise on the table along with a large spoon.

I stare in incomprehension.

"O-oh." Michael wags his finger at me. "I bet you're a Miracle Whip person."

I look at the jar and see the little blue ribbon on the label, the kind of mayonnaise I grew up with. The only kind, in my opinion. My mouth opens. A Miracle Whip person. He as good as called me white trash. What's next, Wonder Bread?

"I knew it!" Michael bounces jauntily back into the kitchen, to return with plates of steaming artichokes and warm, toasty garlic bread.

"You'll know you're back in California when you eat one of these." Michael rips off a large leaf after discarding the small ones around the stem. He dips it in mayo, puts it in his mouth, and then shreds it by pulling it out between his teeth.

I fight tears. I try not to cry continually. And it's become another thing I dislike about me. A bus will belch diesel and I'll be transported back to Madison Avenue. But San Francisco and reality always intrude.

I can't get high. Having little money and no local connections keeps me clean. Just one time, one shot, one line even, and I'll be able to laugh, to not see Voodoo's blown apart head or Pyro's blue feet. Or X-It and his little shoulder shrug, his wide-set innocent eyes, and ironic tug to the corner of his mouth when something strikes him as funny. Anger bursts up and I dowse it with more strangled tears. Where is he?

"Try one," urges Michael as he throws the remains of an artichoke leaf into a bowl. "They're cooled off now."

I sniff and don't meet Michael's eyes.

Last week I phoned Karisma to get in touch with Crikey. When I called Crikey, he'd heard about the deaths and the fire, but had not heard from X-It. I then phoned the organic grocery, but X-It had not come in to work since that day. I left Michael's number. X-It has truly disappeared. Perhaps he went home? I'll write to his parents, when I can remember the address.

I reach out to spoon some mayonnaise from the jar onto my plate. My arm stretches out past my sleeve, revealing my skin. I need shirts with longer sleeves.

Art pushes away from the table, revulsion plain on his face. After a moment of staring at no one and saying nothing, Art gets up and goes out to the hallway. Michael excuses himself and follows him. I can hear their conversation.

"She's worse than picking up a stray cat, Michael. Then we'd only be dealing with fleas and ringworm," Art's voice sounds strained. "She's a drug addict."

"She hasn't done drugs since she got here."

"How do you know? You can't trust her."

Michael's voice has that lovely calm quality I've come to know on the telephone. "I think I can."

"You can't. She's a drug addict."

I've had enough, and shout from the dining table, "The only reason I went out with you is because you looked like a junkie. POSER!"

"That's it," says Art. "I'm out of here. Frank said I could move in with him."

"Don't be rash. Can we talk?" Michael pauses. "Who's Frank?"

"New drummer. And no we can't talk. I'm not gonna live where I'm worried some junkie bitch will steal me blind. I'll be back tomorrow for my stuff. Make sure she doesn't touch it." He slaps the wall. "See ya."

"Art, come on…"

"Enjoy, Mike. And by the way." He raises his voice and directs it at the dining room, "She's horrible in bed."

The front door closes and Michael returns to finish dinner. "I suppose you heard that?"

I nod, a spiny artichoke leaf between my lips.

"Are you?" he asks.

"No," I say.

He cocks his head. "So you're not a drug addict?"

"No." I toss the leaf into the bowl. "I'm not a Miracle Whip person."

* * *

Michael has to work the next day. I bum around San Francisco, and decide to take the bus out to the Tower Records store on Haight Street. Even though I have little funds, looking for Japanese import singles of The Damned beckons as a pleasant way to waste time until Michael finishes work. We have plans to meet outside the Museum of Modern Art on Van Ness.

Flipping through the singles in the record store, I quickly grow bored. Soon, I stop reading the titles and create a percussion pattern by alternating the fingers I use to flip the records, left, left, right. A guy sporting a leather jacket and mohawk walks down the next aisle in front of me.

I spin around. Perhaps Dogbite didn't see me. Heavy, unlaced skinhead boots clomp around the corner.

"J.J.?"

I bare my teeth in a smile of sorts.

Dogbite looks me up and down, taking in Michael's baggy plain jeans, tee shirt, and sneakers. "So the toast of New York got burnt?"

"Hello Dogbite."

He says, "Shame about Voodoo."

"Right." I return to flipping the singles.

"Word is you saw him dead?"

I nod and Dogbite looks at me with newfound respect. Before glancing away, I notice his skin is dirty and too red, like a street person's.

"Sorry about Pyro," I say, figuring simple and direct is best. "When did you come back to SF?"

"Last week. Staying at some chick's place."

"Oh." My earlier flight from New York loses a bit of its melodramatic appeal. "Are the Mod Sisters still in New York?"

"No. London. Wanna come over?"

No. But I say, "Okay." What else am I going to do until five o'clock?

He leads the way, boots galumphing and laces flapping, to a dingy apartment that faces the Panhandle of Golden Gate Park. Inside, dark lace scarves with long fringes grace every available surface and window. Ironically, while the place resembles a vampire brothel, crucifixes hang from the sconces, chandelier, and candlesticks.

"I know, it's a bit frilly,"says Dogbite. "I'm dying to spray-paint a swastika right over there." He points to a wide swath of violet, velvet, Victorian wallpaper.

I spend the afternoon with him, eating Ruffles potato chips and listening to the Sisters of Mercy.

"Where are you crashing?" asks Dogbite.

I haven't thought of staying at Michael's in just that way, but I can't avoid the harsh truth.

"At a friend of Art Munny's."

"That guy who phoned sometimes?" asks Dogbite.

"Yeah." For a second, I wonder what Michael will think of me being here with Dogbite then push the thought away. "We're going to the MOMA at five."

Dogbite brightens a bit. "Mind if I tag along?"

What can I say? His sister died. "Fine."

It isn't like this is a date with Michael or anything. Dogbite jumps up.

"To view art properly, one must be in the proper mindset." He opens a drawer in a black-lacquered Chinese chest and brings meth, syringes, spoon to the coffee table.

I panic. "You can't shoot up and follow me to the museum."

"I'll leave first."

Dogbite tosses a tiny wad of cotton into the spoon and draws up the clear liquid into a syringe.

"But you can't," I protest. My insides twist. "Not without me."

I roll up my sleeve.

Dogbite laughs, sounding uncannily like Voodoo.

*　*　*

I exit the bus, closely followed by Dogbite, and stand on the opposite side of the street from the museum. Perched on a low wall that borders the museum's marble stairs, Michael waits for me. He hasn't spotted me yet, so I watch him. His hands cradle a box. Struck by how vulnerable he looks—like a man afraid of heights who must jump to save his life—I almost do not cross to meet him. Can I stand to see Michael end up as more of my life's wreckage?

Dogbite grabs my elbow, singing, "We're off to see the paintings..." accompanied by a Yellow-Brick-Road skip along the crosswalk.

Michael looks up. His neat dark eyebrows come together. He'll think me a coward, that I need reinforcements. I meet Michael's eyes briefly. How can I hide my condition from him? Suddenly sick, I wonder why that didn't occur to me before?

"Hi, Michael. This is Dogbite. I ran into him in the Haight."

Michael now looks like a man who has gathered the courage to jump from the burning building only to watch the firefighters below move away and take their safety net with them. Dogbite punches him on the arm in lieu of a greeting. We go inside.

Michael carries his box with him throughout the exhibit. The rooms swelter, and I sit down on every available bench, fighting the nausea that rises every few minutes. I was so wrong when I thought doing drugs again would help. I don't feel like Holly Golightly, I feel like I have the flu. What the hell did Dogbite give me?

"Hey," Dogbite whispers. "The crystal's on the house, but you gotta pay for the works. It was brand new. Still in the wrapper. Five bucks." He holds out his hand.

I force a rubbery hand into my jeans pocket, remove a five-dollar bill, and hand it to him.

"I miss her." He sways. "Pyro, I mean. Why couldn't it have been you?" He staggers and refuses to keep his steel-toed boots behind the white lines. The docent asks him to leave. Dogbite whips a can of spray paint out of his army jacket. Security guards whisk him away with alarming speed and less fuss.

Michael walks over and sits next to me. "What do you think of this Rothko?"

I burp.

The painting in front of me wavers. Its pretty horizontal stripes shine in fall colors. "I think he should have designed clothes."

Michael gives a gentle snort. "I take that as a slam?"

"No," I say wistfully, sliding along the wall a bit further. "He would have designed the most bee-u-ti-ful sweaters." That thought brings X-It to mind. Pain wracks my diaphragm, and stomach acid rises at the back of my throat.

"Are you okay?" he asks me.

My secret threatens to jump up and expose me. I'm high.

The docent approaches, stern and gray-haired in a navy blue suit. "Perhaps if the young lady isn't feeling well, it would be best if you folks went home?"

* * *

Michael's bedroom contains a fireplace with an ornate Victorian mantle. On the mantle rests the box he carried throughout the museum. I sit propped on pillows in his bed, looking about at his possessions, gleaning what insights I can from them. A framed Residents poster graces one wall and one of The Talking Heads the other. He has a lovely collection of finely crafted wooden boxes. A large bookcase contains a larger collection of books on the existentialists, Jungian philosophy, art history, and a few on metaphysics.

Michael enters with a bowl of chicken soup on a tray. He places the tray on my lap and then sits down carefully at the foot of the bed.

I take a few sips.

"Feeling any better?" he asks.

"I should be in a bit. This broth is good."

I attempt to slurp quietly. For several long minutes my sips and swallows fill the space between us. He looks at the floor.

"Michael, what's in that box you were carrying this afternoon?"

He stands, fetches it, and then sets it down on the bed. After lifting the tray to the floor, he places the box on my lap. Cedar and rectangular, the box resembles the other ones in his collection.

"It's for you," he says.

Oh gawd, he brought me a present and I brought Dogbite on drugs. I open the box.

Paintbrushes lay nestled on a piece of thick felt.

"They're Winsor Newtons, the finest watercolor brushes made. I took a class but don't use them." He laughs nervously. "I think I was more interested in the art supplies than in making art."

"These are for me?"

"Yes, but they come with a very big string attached."

I brace. Here it is. I absolutely cannot sleep with Michael. I like him too much, as a friend.

"You have to use them in art school."

I let out a very audible sigh of relief. Michael puts two and two together in about the same number of seconds. He looks hurt.

I close the box. He takes it from me and places it on the nightstand. Sitting down, so close our hips touch, he braces himself by putting a hand down on the other side of me. His arm and torso bridge my body.

I tense. "I can't." Frantic now, I repeat, "I can't."

He takes my left arm in his hands and turns it palm upward. I shiver as his hair tickles my skin and he places a light kiss right on the track mark. Hopefully he didn't see it. Michael touches his index finger to my lips. He then tucks the strands of my hair that are long enough behind my ears.

Matter-of-factly he says, "Move over." He smiles. "Come on, scoot."

I don't move and prepare to make a dash for the couch in the living room. He jumps over my body, surprising a little, "Ooh," from me. Once on my other side, he settles his pillows, my pillows, and then pulls the blanket over my shoulders. He remains on top of the covers.

"Turn off the light."

I do. He settles down.

"Come here."

"Michael…" Tears threaten again.

He pulls me close and holds me tightly, so very tightly he becomes my outer shell.

"Go on. I've got you."

"Wha—?" I choke back a sob. I realize I'm nestled in the sheets that I heard rustling so many times on the phone.

"Go on and cry." His lips brush my ear. "I'm not letting go."

Much later, I wake, fully clothed and still in Michael's arms. He's asleep. I blink, my eyes scratchy and sore. My ribs ache from sobbing. I look about the room in the dark. Headlight trails cross the ceiling like glimmers of hope.

The inside of my elbow is sore, a reminder of my relapse. Here in the sanity of Michael's arms, my actions this afternoon make no sense. But he can't hold me everywhere I go, can he?

He stirs. "You awake?"

"Mmm-hmm."

He strokes my hair. "There's something very special about you, Juliana. I noticed it right when I met you at your going away party. Not only are you beautiful. You have sparkle. And guts. But, if you ever take drugs again, you are out of my apartment, and my life."

He knows. He knew at the museum, at home, when he brought me soup, when he kissed my arm. I laugh inwardly, deriding myself. How could he not have known? But still, he holds me now, and offers another chance.

My heart and soul belong to X-It. But as long as I don't know where X-It is, I might stay here, and prove to Michael his faith in me isn't misplaced. I reach out and stroke the box of watercolor brushes.

"Thank you," I say.

CHAPTER TWENTY-SIX

San Francisco
October, 1981

Except for the hole X-It left, I am feeling better than I have in a long while. Michael feeds me well, and makes me laugh. Tonight we made stuffed chicken breasts. Now we're horsing around. Michael grabs Russ's tape I brought back from New York.

"Give it back," I say. My memories are clear enough, no need to watch the tape.

There is a permanent ache where X-It is supposed to be, a ghost limb, a war wound bestowed by an almost-lover. Unlike old wounds that worsen in the rain, a shower of tears drives away this pain. For a while, anyway. But the longer I stay with Michael, the less I cry. And then I find myself missing the ache.

"Come on, I wanna see it," he pleads mischievously then holds the tape overhead and out of reach.

"No. It's humiliating." I sink down into the couch, physically admitting defeat.

He pops the videotape into a special Beta player he borrowed. Plopping down next to me, he reaches over and hands me a glass of red wine.

The tape plays. Strobe lights alternate with black lights, revealing ultraviolet Dance-o-Matic club patrons. The camera scans their faces, stops, and then focuses on each portrait I painted of the fallen Rock icons.

"Those are pretty good." He nudges me with his elbow. I shift quickly to avoid spilling wine on his sofa.

The patrons, resplendent in New York underground tribal blacklight paint, commence to shred, tear, and mutilate my paintings, stomping on the bits that fall to the floor.

Penny's beautiful face flashes by, and X-It's.

I grip the arm of the couch. Cold seeps under my clothes as I recall sitting on the pier that night. I shiver.

He looks at my face.

"I'm sorry." He puts his arm around my shoulder. I place my wine glass on the coffee table, and as I lean forward his hand slides down my back. "Those brainless twits tore up your paintings, but there might be a way to salvage them."

"What do you mean?" I look away from a glimpse of X-It's unique features.

"It's visually exciting, isn't it? Look at the tape, at the whole incident, as a work of art, a performance."

Michael turns his entire body to face me, his knee presses into the back cushions. Glad of a bit of physical distance, I sigh and pick up my glass. Michael doesn't press me for sex. Ever.

He says, "When I asked you to apply to art school, you filled out the paperwork but didn't turn it in, right?"

I hate it when he plays dad. "Because I didn't have a portfolio. I don't have any art to submit."

Michael points at the screen. "Yes you do. In fact, this might even be better. You can call it a video performance piece of a live installation."

"What?" How can a computer guy be so arty?

He jumps up and, despite my best preventive efforts, several drops of wine land on the upholstery. I set my glass on the end table. I don't want wine anyway. I don't want drugs either, and have been clean since the art museum. The better I feel, the better I want to feel. I am now greedy for health. Only I don't know how much damage I may have done.

Michael answers, "I know a woman who works in the admissions office at the Art Institute. With the right approach, she'll flip for it. And for you."

I see spilled coffee flooding the desk and papers at Parsons. I cringe.

"Aw come on, it's not that scary."

He pulls me up to him unexpectedly. Lips crush mine. Not ready, not ready, rush my thoughts. But he smells good. Fresh, human and spicy.

With his lips still on mine, his hands violently untuck my shirt from my pants.

I pull my lips away. "Michael, I was a dirty junkie. What about, you know, disease?"

Michael keeps me pressed tightly to him and works his hands under my shirt. His fingers feel marvelous along my back.

"You're not using that excuse again tonight." Freed from my lips, his mouth traverses my neck and he mumbles, light-hearted, "We'll take the same precautions we would to prevent anything else."

Sunk, I dare to touch him. Steel-cable muscles along either side of his spine surprise me. His arms prove to be sinewy, with the points of his shoulders and collar bones protruding. The tensile strength of his torso shocks me.

Michael gathers me up and carries me to the bedroom. As he lowers me to the bed, his lips brush my sternum just over my heart.

"Let me love you. Just let me love you."

On the surface it sounds like a simple request. But I've never managed it in all my previous sexual encounters.

But my body responds. Every hair follicle, every pore, every nerve comes alive. My clothes are off. Michael kneels, bare-chested in black jeans, towering above me. His gaze roams every inch of me. My skin reacts to his visual adoration. I can feel his eyes move upon me.

"You are so beautiful," he murmurs, "like a small, perfect statue."

He admires me with his hands, his fingertips, his mouth. My starving body pushes my mind aside and accepts his love. As I rise on a swirling cloud of passion that I swear is colored pink, my last translatable thought bubbles up and dissipates, *I can feel.*

And as his body merges with mine I surrender to this soul-filling pleasure, pulling him more deeply into me, eager to delight him the same way. Overwhelmed, drowning, I don't know what I should do now. His body floats above mine like a life raft. I wrap both arms about his ribs and hold on.

CHAPTER TWENTY-SEVEN

San Francisco
December 25, 1981

Morning sunlight travels through the Golden Gate and slants into the kitchen of Michael's apartment, where our new kittens mill about my feet. Hoping not to wake Michael, I quietly fill the coffeepot to surprise him with Christmas coffee in bed.

With steaming mug in hand, I pad back toward the bedroom, stopping to gaze in at the living room. The kittens shoot past my ankles and bound toward the tree. Michael and I brought the little noble fir home, set it on the tabletop, and adorned it with popcorn, ribbons, and a single ornament. The German mercury glass pickle, Michael's choice, glints in the sun, symbolic of our first Christmas together.

I shoo away the cats as they tug at the tassels on the table cloth. A package lies tucked under the bottom branches. I catch my breath. After setting down Michael's coffee, I run to the hall closet and retrieve my present for him and add it to his under the tree. How wonderful he put my present out at night, like Santa Claus. I pick up his coffee and stride to the bedroom.

Michael's drowsy face appears from under the comforter. Eyes half closed, his fingers motion for me to come into his outstretched arms.

After coffee, we open presents.

"You first," says Michael.

Excited, yet shy and feeling a bit undeserving, I hesitate. He hands me a pretty package with pink and green striped paper. I self consciously strip bow and paper from the box.

"Ah," I exclaim as a new purse, an actual purse not a duffle, falls into my lap. "It's cute!" And it is.

Michael eagerly tears into his slim package.

"An 'I Heart New York' mouse pad." He laughs. "Very funny." He immediately sets the mouse pad in its place of honor next to his beloved Commodore Amiga computer.

* * *

Later that day, I scrunch in the corner of the couch next to the fireplace in Michael's parents' home. Half-hidden by the spreading branches of the enormous tree, I observe the Danner Family Christmas.

The clunk of billiard balls tells me Michael still plays in the "rumpus room," as the Danners call it, with his brother. Grandpa Danner, in his nineties and smelling of the same pipe tobacco my dad tried to smoke last Christmas, sits right down next to me.

"You're Michael's new friend?" He leans in.

Michael's mother, Mary Danner, clutches a bowl of Holiday potpourri and comes to my aid. "This is Juliana, Dad. She's going to go to art school."

"I start in January," I say with a stronger grin than I feel.

Mary sets down the potpourri on the mantle. "Dinner's in five minutes. Why don't you round up the kids from the rumpus room, Juliana?"

I poke my head into the room that houses a billiard table, young Danners around pinball and foosball games, and a dart board on a pockmarked, wood-paneled wall.

"I've been asked to fetch you for dinner," I say.

Michael ignores me as he aims and takes his shot. The blue-striped ball misses the corner pocket.

He sighs, rubs his stomach. "Good."

Michael chases me down the hall after his herd of young relations. We tumble into the crowded dining room breathless and red-faced, and then squeeze amongst the tables.

"Everyone, be seated," says Mary as she lights long red tapers in holly-draped candlesticks.

The Danner Family Christmas Dinner makes me want to cry. Is X-It eating cold ham with wet Persian cats in his family's refrigerator garden?

I sit upright. This family could be my family. As dinner wears on, members of the family swap Christmas stories. I mostly smile, sip my wine, and try to keep a straight face as Michael's secret glances become increasingly suggestive. Then I hear my name and drop my fork.

"Never mind, Juliana, I'll get you another," says Mary. "Can you share a Christmas story with us?"

"Uh…"

"It doesn't have to be anything special," says Aunt Hypochondria.

"Yeah," says Daniel, Michael's brother, "Just tell us what you did last Christmas."

"Or Christmas in a past life," Mary says and grins as her husband looks to the ceiling in mock exasperation.

That explains the metaphysical books on Michael's shelf, they came from his mom.

Grandpa Danner pours me more wine. His pipe tobacco takes me right back to Philadelphia. I glance at Michael. His face reassures me, although it holds expectation: tell a story, it says, and walk through the Danner Family door, or refuse to tell a story and stay outside.

I drink half my glass of wine, clear my throat, and the story of last Christmas comes swimming out of my mouth. All Danner eyes are upon me as I recount the lit match in the dog's fur, Jack yelling at me, Mim with her tea, cigarettes, and Jean Naté cologne, Pip and his protective memory loss. To shield young Danner ears, I leave out the part about my dad leering at me in the pool and my having to leave the house for his sex therapist. After the parts about the muskrat, and brunch and the Baptist Church, I'm finally retelling kneeling at the bridge in front of my pyramid of fruitcakes.

"And what did you do?" asks Grandpa earnestly.

"I set them on fire," I say.

The entire Danner clan, all sixteen of them not counting the kids' table, sit in stunned silence.

Mary wipes her eyes and says, "I believe Juliana gets the prize this year. Who has it?"

"I do," says Conspiracy Theory cousin. He ambles off to get it and returns.

"Prize for what?" I ask, hardly believing I spilled my guts like that.

"For the best Christmas story," says Michael's dad with a wink.

The cousin hands me a heavy box the size and shape of a brick.

"It gets passed around every year," says Mary.

A Christmas pattern decorates the cardboard. I lift the lid. An ancient, cellophane-wrapped fruitcake stares back at me.

And I laugh, honest and true, possibly for the first time.

Next comes the tradition I've dreaded since Michael told me about the Danner family Christmas get-together: The present exchange.

All Danners file into the living room and settle on furniture, footstools, and the floor. I choose the hearth. The fire crackles merrily, and Burl Ives sings holiday tunes in the background.

Luckily, they chose Secret Santa names out of a hat last year, so I figure the whole uncomfortable process should take less than an hour. Mary and the aunt bring in trays of hot cocoa and cookies, and as a young niece hands out the presents from a basket, the Danners sing carols along with Burl Ives.

Michael moves to be near me and puts a hand on my knee. He sings out bravely, although he clearly hasn't much of a voice. I tentatively join in. At first he looks surprised at the pleasing tones coming from my small person, and then he grins and puts his arm around me.

The niece stops in front of Michael and hands him an envelope. She turns to me and places a small box in my lap.

"Michael!" I hiss in protest, "You told me I shouldn't bring a gift."

My present is very light, giving me the impression of fragility, and as I open it I know I'm correct.

"Oh, Michael, look," I say as I hold it aloft, and then wish I hadn't spoken. Mary gave me a Christmas ornament. Two painted French harlequins, Pierrot and Pierrette, lean in for a kiss under mistletoe. Above them are the words, "Love is Forever." Mary has given me the most frightening gift imaginable, but I can't imagine parting with it.

Back at Michael's apartment later that evening, I take the harlequin ornament from its box and hang it next to the pickle on the small Noble fir. I pick up my new purse and decide to start using it right away. After I transfer the contents of my duffle into the purse, I turn my old canvas bag upside down and shake it. An object, creepy and familiar, falls out. Fear shoots straight to the soles of my feet.

A black yarn trouble doll.

"Michael!" I scream.

He thuds down the hall and careens through the door. I point to the object.

"It's Voodoo's trademark." I try to catch my breath.

"You know," he says poking at it. "It's kinda cute."

He looks at the expression on my face and stops kidding.

In a dead-on imitation of Glinda the Good Witch of the North, he says, "Begone, you have no power here," and pinches the yarn doll between his fingers.

He then minces to the toilet as if wearing high heels and flushes the offending object.

Behind him, I laugh. Tears run down my face. Michael is so funny, so secure in his masculinity, yet something about his comic walk reminds me of Voodoo in his flamenco boots. Michael wraps his arms about me.

"We can be happy together." He sighs deeply. "Just let me make you happy."

The toilet gurgles as the tank refills.

I vow to get super healthy again. Tomorrow I will start a daily running regimen and take a run down to the Polk Street pier. Maybe I can borrow Michael's Walkman.

"I want to make you happy too." I smile.

He scoops me up with obvious lascivious intent. "Oh, that's easy."

CHAPTER TWENTY-EIGHT

I run. Each foot strikes the pavement to the beat of the song in the Sony Walkman. *"Let's get phy-si-cal, phy-si-cal…"* Olivia Newton John's breathy voice sings her new release. I smile and allow the unabashed pop song to push me along. Now that I don't care about punk, post-punk or new-wave anymore, I can listen to any damn song I choose.

Besides, it's Michael's Walkman. He thinks Olivia is sexy.

Winter sun glares off the cement as I speed north. At the crest, I ease. There, blue and cool, spreads the San Francisco Bay. Spurred on by the intoxicating sea air, I tear downhill, once more a child speeding out of control. The tall masts of the museum ships nestled in their moorings far below at the base of Polk Street look like hypodermic needles. And I don't give a shit.

At the pier, I take a sharp left and turn my entire focus toward ascending the steep hill that leads to the Fort Mason park. Struggling to run like I used to, I breathe in and breathe out. My consciousness becomes my breath, my thighs, and the blur of asphalt beneath my feet. This makes room in my psyche for something else, something big. Something wrong. Horribly wrong.

I yank off the headphones. My feet falter and find their way to the cement wall above the rocks and water fifty feet below. Bottle-green water rises and swells against the wall, breaking around the rocks. White salt suds and bubbles skim the surface, like scum on top of a boiling soup pot.

I suck in great gulps of air tinged with smells of saltwater and seaweed and try to figure out what's wrong. I grab the wall.

"Don't give up now!" calls a fellow female jogger who toils up the incline a short distance behind me.

I flap a small thanks. With small penguin steps, the tired runner tops the rise and disappears around the corner.

The message presses with insistence like a giant cotton ball against the side of my brain. I look out to the Golden Gate, the Marin headlands, and beyond, as if he is out there, not in New York, three thousand miles in the opposite direction. It's X-It, calling me for help.

Layered in salt and sweat, I rush back back to Michael's apartment. I fumble for the key on the string around my neck. Victorian dust motes, floating for a hundred years, swirl about my nostrils as I let myself in along with a shaft of light. The kittens pad toward me down the hallway lined in pressed tin, painted white. I ignore their appeals for food and bee-line for the blinking answering machine. After pushing the replay button, I feed the kittens while waiting for the cassette to rewind.

The sharp edge of the cat food can lid bites into my finger as the answering machine beeps and a watery, whining voice speaks, "Hello— my name is Linden—you don't know me." The voice coughs, as if it has all the time in the world. I press blood from my finger into the aluminum kitchen sink to flush out the wound. I remember Voodoo washing my cut finger the first time I visited Penny's loft.

The message continues, "I work with Thomas at the Sunrise Health Food Market. Strictly produce, you know. I don't cashier. Thomas asked me to call you. He's sick. Real sick. He's at St. Jude's, the county place, you know, where you go when you can't pay. He wants to see—" The tape cuts him off.

I curse. No other message appears, but I don't need one. X-It is dying and wants to see me.

When Michael's key turns in the lock, his suitcase lays open on the bed, half-packed with my things.

"You're home!" I try to sound like my usual self.

"Yup." The smile, which fills his face as soon as he sees me, falls away the instant he looks behind me to the suitcase.

"I'm going to New York. I'll be back Saturday."

"This is rather sudden, isn't it?" His neat eyebrows come together. "What about the Art Institute?"

"I'll be back before the semester starts. X-It's in the hospital. He's dying. He asked for me."

"Don't go." He runs his fingers through his swept back hair. It feels like something bad is going to happen."

He wrestles a bag of garbage out the back door that leads to the stairwell. The kittens, who watch me pack, jump off of the bed and trot toward the Pied-Piper call of the open door. I watch their retreating tails.

"I'll be back Saturday," I repeat to the kitchen and throw a pair of socks into the suitcase with too much force.

I hear his voice from outside, "My mother told me you'd leave. Said I could fix up a broken bird but it would fly away."

My love for X-It is embedded, like the flesh of a tree grown over a tight rope. "I have to go. But I'm coming back."

"Okay." He stands behind me.

I touch the cut on my finger. "He's dying."

"Yup." His voice sounds like our relationship just died. He doesn't believe I'm coming back.

* * *

The moving sidewalk glides through the tunnel that connects the parking garage to the airport terminal. Standing backwards, I clutch his borrowed backpack with one arm and hold the moving handrail with the other. Michael grows smaller and smaller. He gave me a ride to the airport but refused to walk me to the gate. I can still make out his Buddy Holly glasses. He stands there until I'm out of sight, looking like he might follow me. But he won't.

CHAPTER TWENTY-NINE

New York City

The only thought on my mind as I exit Penn Station is also the only thought I had on the airplane. I must get to X-It.

Every movie scene where a person races to the hospital only to find an empty bed replays in my mind. I heft my bag and cross the street to take a taxi uptown to St. Jude's

I stop at the front reception desk and ask what room Thomas Leavitt occupies. As I exit the elevator I'm enveloped by the smells of sebum on unwashed skin and floor cleaner. I associate hospitals with my father and find them disturbing.

X-It sleeps as I enter the room. His roommate, an elderly man, watches a game show on television. The remote control he was pointing at the T.V. in the corner now jabs at me.

"I want a different room. Tell them to move me. He's going to die in here and I don't want to be here when he does."

"Excuse me?"

"Stinks of death," shouts the patient, who appears to be as healthy as possible for an old guy in a hospital gown. He draws the curtain around his bed with a flourish, and I turn my attention to X-It.

But it's not him. The man in the bed is someone else.

A nurse enters, checks the chart belonging to the inert form, and turns to leave.

"Is there a doctor available?" I startle the nurse. People often don't see me now that I have brown hair.

"He'll be in shortly. Are you family?" She looks hopeful.

I shake my head.

I pull up the padded hospital chair and observe the drips from the IV take their roller coaster rides down into the back of the patient's hand as it lies limp on the bed. When the doctor enters, it's obvious the nurse alerted him to my presence.

"Um, Doctor, I'm looking for Thomas Leavitt. I was told he was here." Please God don't let this be X-It, he's unrecognizable.

"And you are?"

"J.J. Buckingham."

"Ah, Mr. Leavitt was asking for you. He left the hospital earlier today."

"You released him?" I ask.

"No I did not. He left. I'm afraid his condition isn't good. You must prepare yourself for a possible negative outcome."

I live my life braced for possible negative outcomes. "What exactly is his condition?"

"Septicemia. Blood infection."

"Is there anything you can do?" I sound desperate.

"Not unless he checks himself back in for treatment." He clicks his pen against X-It's chart and leaves the room.

I can't help thinking that the doctor's tone hints that treatment would be a waste of money, taxpayer's money in X-It's case, which is ironic, because X-It never filed a tax return in his life.

He's one of those people who slip through the cracks with naïve defiance. X-It slipped away from me, through the cracks a final time.

I locate some lotion and shake it out onto my hands. I rub them together until they hurt.

I'm up. My shoes squeak. Stub my toes, going too fast. Hallways and gurneys and grey faces flash by me. I want out.

How could he leave the hospital? Stupid X-It.

I take the subway downtown, get off at Union Square and walk down St. Mark's. I try to calm down and breathe.

I look so different now, I doubt any biker would recognize me. The food smells are much the same, falafel and curry and burgers. The sidewalk is still cracked in the same places.

Three made-to-look-like-vintage clothing stores have popped up since I left. Studded belts glint at me from a display window as I pass. Their scuffed and dirty mannequin wears a magenta Mohawk wig and pre-shredded tights. A sign says the tights are eight dollars on sale. Looks like I left New York just in time.

But I'm here. Back. A passing reflection on the glass looks like Michael's woeful face. I keep moving.

I reach the painted portal of Sphinx. Trash blows by my feet. The sign on the door advertises the space for lease. No more Sphinx, no more tall, tiny-dreadlocked bartender.

Demolition noise makes me turn around to look down Fifth street, to my old home. The fire energized someone with a big bankroll. Cranes and bulldozers attack buildings on both sides of the street. Clawfuls of bricks and plaster land in the giant bin and the life stories of immigrants, hippies, and junkies float away with the dust.

X-It isn't here. There's no way I can find him. Pure instinct drove me down here.

For lack of anywhere else to go, I head west, toward Chelsea and our pier. Of course X-It won't be sitting out there, sick, but I go anyway.

On Eighth Avenue a bus bears down on the stoplight and I step back from the curb. It passes. I look up and see the bakery across the street.

Inside the window, Eileen smiles as she hands a crisp white bag and cup of coffee to a customer. Her clean apron matches her scrubbed face.

I dash across the avenue. Taxis honk.

My face prickles with sudden heat as I push through the door into the warmth of the bakery. The customer edges around me to leave and Eileen straightens.

"J.J!" She wipes spotless hands on her pristine apron. "I certainly never expected to see you again."

I shrug and inspect the bearclaw

"You look good. I mean great. Really healthy." Pink-cheeked, Eileen leans partway over the counter to inspect all of me. "You are er, healthy, right?"

I laugh. "Yeah."

She nods and then reaches into the case for a bearclaw. "You know, if you were to stay healthy permanently, I bet you could get your job back." A steamy coffee joins the bearclaw on top of the case. She pushes them toward me. "You like your coffee light, right?

"Yes, thanks." Wow, she remembered.

"We haven't had a counter girl as good as you since you left."

Despite all my better instincts, I smile.

"Oh, wait!" Eileen shuffles off to the kitchen and then returns, waving an envelope. "This came here for you."

I take the letter not knowing what to expect. Has my mom divorced Martin and taken up with a quadriplegic guy?

With the letter wrapped around the coffee cup, I back away from the counter. The awkward moment of parting is interrupted by three kids coming in for an after-school snack.

I wave the bearclaw as a goodbye to Eileen but her attention is already on serving up brownies.

Before the door shuts completely, I hear her shout, "You're a good girl, J.J."

At the end of the rotting pier, I enjoy the coffee and some of the bearclaw before opening the letter. I turn it over. It's not from my mom.

The return address says it came from Mim. I unfold the letter and catch something that flutters out.

A voucher for a train ticket. To go to Philadelphia.

Dear Juliana,

Your father asked me to write to you. (Yeah, right.) *Since you didn't bother to give us an address I looked up the bakery where you said you were working. I hope this gets to you.*

It is your father's greatest wish that he help you attend university and acquire a degree that will get you a well-paying career. We would like you to come and live with us while you apply to schools in the area. Acceptable majors are business, law, or the sciences. Your father will not pay for a degree in English, philosophy, or the arts.

After you graduate, we will help you secure an apartment in the area. This letter should prove to you our love and generosity. I only hope you are sensible enough to accept it.

Please call us when you arrive and Pip will pick you up. Do not allow him to stop at the store on the way home.

Awaiting you with open arms,
Your grandmother

Mim can't be serious. Go to Good Girl U? My boot knocks the rest of my pastry into the water with a cold splash. Screw Mim. I've earned a PhD in Bad Girl and I'll see where it takes me.

By mistake I bite the side of my mouth. My tongue comforts the wound. The Danners couldn't be more different from Mim and company. I am sensible enough to see that love doesn't ask for anything in return.

What I want to do for X-It is what Michael did for me. J.J. Buckingham, Bad Girl Saint.

I tuck the ticket voucher inside the folded pages and place the letter in my backpack, which feels heavier than it did on my way to the hospital. The sky darkens, anchored by low winter clouds. Snow clouds. If I were to paint them I'd use Payne's Gray and a touch of Naples Yellow.

The giant neon coffee cup across the river lights up. The drop-drop-drops must be burned out because they remain dark. I gather my things and go.

After a supper of chicken soup at Veselka's, I wander around freezing until ten p.m. Outside Dance-O-Matic there is no line of eager clubgoers waiting to get in. I walk straight up, pay my money, and am allowed inside, where the blaring music is trying too hard.

Russ leans against the elevator talking to a couple of older guys in suits. I think it's Russ. Yeah it is, he looks different because he's wearing a suit Not an embroidered Rockabilly suit, not a Mod suit with narrow lapels, but a SUIT suit. His trademark swoop is combed flat and shiny like the acrylic wigs on the male mannequins at my old job.

Moving closer I can hear what he's saying, "So the best timing to go condo is in the spring? Why don't we go ahead and put a retainer on a contractor?"

The other suits mumble. I can't make out their words.

Russ says, "Well let's get some bids then. I'm an investor now and I say let's move on this."

I try to maneuver by them to get to the staircase. A hand falls on my shoulder and spins me around.

"J.J?"

"Russ, hello."

"Wow, you look incredible."

"Thanks. You too." I turn to ascend the stairs and look over my shoulder. My throat tightens as I ask, "Have you seen X-It?"

"No, but Hot Toddy is tending bar on the Fourth Floor."

I give him the slightest of nods and head upstairs, feeling his gaze on my back until I'm out of his sight.

I breeze through the doorway of the Fourth Floor and make a beeline for the bar. "Hey, bartender," I call out to the fey creature whose face is obscured by a curtain of dark hair as he bends to scoop ice cubes.

He shoots upright in indignation and then softens when he sees me. After jamming the scoop back into the ice, he sways over to my side of the bar. He pours me an expensive whiskey and slides it under my nose.

"So why are you slinging instead of spinning?" I ask. I don't really care, but I have to say something before demanding to know where X-It is.

"Penance for not playing The Human League."

I snort, but I don't need to worry that he heard me. It's too noisy in here.

I lean forward on my elbows, hovering over my untouched whiskey. "Have you seen my old roommate?" I practically shout.

"You mean the guy who got his head blown off?" His eyebrows arch. "No."

I frown. "My roommate X-It. White-blond hair. Was a bicycle messenger."

Now Todd's eyebrows pinch together. "He wasn't your roommate. He lived with that Penny girl. The one who moved to London."

"Have you seen him?"

"Not lately. My guess is he's hanging out at Highwire. You know, the club that opened up in the vacant church on Sixth Avenue. Everybody goes there now."

The whiskey is my punishment. I slam the drink and run from the Fourth Floor like it's on fire and not my throat.

CHAPTER THIRTY

After walking right past the velvet rope like I'm Karisma, I pass beneath the gothic door of New York's new hippest club. Highwire stinks. I press my hand to my nose to avoid the smells of vomit and churchliness.

A pulsating dance beat serves as the choir. There are no pews, only writhing bodies. Strobes and violet spotlights take the place of candles. If X-It is here he is in the most exclusive corner of this hell-hole. Eduardo, the semi-famous fashion illustrator, bops by me and I grab his sleeve.

Angling his head he inspects me head to toe. "Oh, if it isn't our barbed wire Holly Golightly? Only now you look, oh I don't know, normal."

I ignore his comment. "Have you seen X-It?"

"Come, come." Eduardo says like he means, *tsk tsk*. "We're up in the choir loft."

We? If Penny is here I'm going to go off like church bells. Electric jolts that have nothing to do with the strobe lights turn my insides to mush. Will X-It be happy to see me?

A turning wooden stairway leads to the loft. After the disco battlefield glare of the dance floor, my eyes adjust to the relative darkness. A few creatures of the night are lounging on tattered velvet cushions and plastic drink cups roll about the floor. I skitter on a stir straw in a puddle of liquid. And there he is. Asleep.

His complexion is so translucent he practically glows in the dark. A wax museum Camille. When we lived together he used to covet the cheeks of young children, and often admonished me to treat my skin like silk. X-It, a lover of Beauty, has little patience with imperfection. And I am all ragged edges. Gently, I touch his face. His eyelids flutter.

"X-It, it's me. I'm here."

His eyelids rise as slowly as heavy velvet drapes at the opera. He takes a moment to focus on me. The absent choir may as well start singing because he is transcendent, beautiful.

"J.J.," he croaks, "You don't look right in brown hair."

"It's my natural color."

"I rest my case." He smiles and his beauty rips apart the seams on everything I'm trying to hold together.

He closes his eyes again and lays still. Intermission? Or final curtain? Afraid he might have permanently rested his case I shake his arm.

"Don't go anywhere," I say. I remember him as he was on his bicycle, fit and in full command. Wetness creeps down my cheeks. My sleeve mops it up.

"Jesus," Eduardo breaks in. "Haven't you ever seen anyone nod off before?"

I startle. I'd forgotten Eduardo was here. "Hey, can I have a few minutes alone with X-It please?"

X-It nods at Eduardo, who backs away a few paces. I pull up a cushion and gingerly sit down.

X-It's eyes open to slits and survey me more closely. "When did you get so fucking healthy?"

I want to ask him when he got so fucking sick, but I say nothing.

He asks, "J.J., are you clean?"

"Yes. I feel great." I swing my arms. "I can run again."

"Yeah?"

I take his question to mean he's interested. "Yeah. I'm clean. I'm thinking straight. I can help you get clean too. Get strong again."

"I'm glad you're here." Cold fingers twine against my sweaty ones and stiffen a moment. "You'll stay in New York now, won't you?"

I smile at him and massage his hand. I can't bear to hurt Michael. But I can't leave X-It, not like this. What if he dies?

"How long have we been friends?" he asks, almost in a whisper.

"A year and a half."

"No," his eyelids slide shut again, "I've known you forever."

"I'll stay." My heart breaks. If I have to sacrifice Michael, and art school, it's what I need to do. I owe it to X-It to save him. I'm the one who messed him up. I lie down next to him and stroke his hair. I swallow. My fingers tremble. What better place to confess this particular sin than in a church turned nightclub? I say, "I'm sorry for shooting you up that first time. I am so sorry, for everything.

"I'll do anything you want, X. I'll dye my hair and sell popsicles in the park. I'll bicycle on Fifth Avenue." I smile at him through tears. With my whole being I want him to get better. I want him to love me. "Come on, X, I love you, just let me take you back to the hospital."

A strange look comes over his face, it might be sadness. "Sure, J.J. But first, hand me my messenger bag."

I hand X-It the bag. His eyes, bioluminescent like a being from the depths, sparkle and burn into mine.

With the crook of his finger, X-It motions Eduardo close to us and whispers, "Don't be sad, J.J. I'll sleep with you if that's what you want. Stay with me. We can party one last time before I get clean." From his bag he withdraws a capped hypodermic filled with brown liquid.

I imagine tying off with my backpack strap, my vein popping up, eager. In my mind, the needle pricks my flesh, a whorl of blood shows in the syringe and I push the plunger to the hilt.

A year ago I wouldn't have hesitated. In my excitement I would have considered it a win-win. Now, the persistent tug makes me feel sick. Bile bursts in my throat.

My hand tenses as I prepare to tear it away, but X-It places my fingers into the semi-famous fashion illustrator's palm.

"Eduardo'll join us." X-It winks at me. "It's the only way this'll work."

I feel like I just rammed face first into a chunk of ice.

He looks incredulous at my reaction. "When Voodoo slept with me he said we'd get you to join in too. And that wasn't my first time shooting up," he says, "Voodoo and the gang partied at Penny's as soon as she signed the lease." He laughs. "We were high when we met up with you for the St. Pat's Parade. Couldn't you tell?"

I should feel exonerated, free. Why am I so angry I want to spew? "But I didn't see track marks."

He shrugs. "It was just a time or two. And Penny's good. She used a lot sharper needle than you did."

Eduardo tosses my hand away. He points to a group of club-goers I don't know, kids even younger than us. "Come on," he says to X-It. "Let's dump this boring pity fuck and go with them."

No sound comes out as my mouth gapes. I am downstairs before I know what happened.

At the altar, I trip over a lone platform boot, but no one sees. I look back toward the loft. He is not going to get clean. I wonder where his portfolio is? Who cares? His talent is meaningless unless he does something with it.

I run out the side door into a small garden area. Raindrops pelt my face as if the gargoyles above are spitting their disapproval. Gothic Halloween decorations hang wet and tattered from the trees even though it's almost New Years. I make my escape through the creaky gate. My scarf catches on the pointed iron fence and yanks me back.

As I work my scarf free of the iron arrow, I know there is only one place left for me now. One place where I haven't fucked up irretrievably. One place that can save me, and possibly one person.

San Francisco. And Michael. But I don't deserve him. He doesn't know what I've been capable of, and I can't bring this kind of mess into his life. *Shit, X-It, really? A pity fuck?* One nasty thought leads me to another, maybe Michael only feels sorry for me?

I have a voucher for train tickets. I can go anywhere. J.J. Buckingham, always flight, never fight.

On Sixth Avenue I hail a taxi and one pulls right over, a fringe benefit of looking normal.

"Grand Central Terminal," I say and burst into tears. Rain slashes at the car windows and I cry cold tears all the way across town. My sobs are so terrible that when the driver pulls to the curb beneath winged Mercury hovering over the Terminal clock, he waves me out with a free fare. Mercury's face, sensuous and aloof, reminds me of X-It's. I was a fool to think X-It could ever love me back. Mercury smirks and I look away. Perhaps X-It knew instinctively that the things I loved most about him were his qualities I wanted to possess.

I can no longer dredge up any emotion regarding X-It. Love, if that's what it was, is gone. Lust and envy are gone. Sympathy is dead. So is anger. I turn away, careful not to call those feelings back. I let him go.

I consider huddling, wet and pathetic, against a marble column until the ticket booth opens. But movement and lights halfway down the block show me a twenty-four hour coffee shop. I wait at the counter in a less cinematic but more civilized fashion, with coffee, Danish, and newspaper.

The sun finally wakes up and the train station employees arrive along with an awful lot of other people. I look around. Michael would love Grand Central and all its weird old stuff, especially the four-faced clock. I need to exchange Mim's voucher for a ticket. I descend the cold stone staircases to where the trains come in. I check the blackboard.

How far can I go for a fare equivalent to Philadelphia? Rhinebeck? Hartford? Atlantic City?

Hungry again, I search the depths of my satchel for that extra donut I snagged at the coffee shop. No wonder my bag is so heavy, it looks like there's a brick at the bottom. I pull it out and recognize the box. The Danner Family Fruitcake. My tears run free. Michael must have put the fruitcake in my bag. I take it out of its box and inhale it's still-sweet aroma. That goofball. That cute, too-good-for-me, goofball.

Tourist brochures are displayed on the counter. A leaflet with a picture of Rockefeller Center catches my eye. The Christmas tree is still up. I should go see it before I leave.

Wait a minute. I don't have to leave. I don't have to run away. I am giddy with the truth of it. I can stay in New York, get a room at the Y, get my job at the bakery back. I can work on a portfolio and apply to Parsons. I can show Michael that I can be deserving of him. I suddenly need to be at Rockefeller Center, right in the middle of this goddam city, to get New York's blessing.

I race up through the bowels of Grand Central Terminal, across the Main Concourse, and out the doors beneath Mercury's gaze. Outside, the rain has turned to snow. New Yorkers bustle down the sidewalk in both directions, mostly oblivious to the softly falling magic.

Michael's backpack bangs against my back as I take off running. I thread my way past Madison and then up Fifth Avenue, where I have a straight five block distance to Forty-ninth Street. Frigid air laced with scents of roasting chestnuts and wet wool blows my soul clean. Snowflakes kiss my face. Shit, a red light. For the first time I am one of those New York pedestrians who play chicken with the taxis. I make it.

I grin when I reach the Rockefeller Center shopping promenade that leads to the edge of the skating rink below. I reach the wall and look down on golden Prometheus and the skaters. I am going to be just fine. Exultant, I turn around and watch the tourists.

A man facing away from me wears a jacket that's all wrong for this weather and it flaps like the flags above. Hands tucked under his arms, he turns and graces the skaters with a sad scowl. I catch a glimpse of horned-rim glasses.

I reach into my pack and then tap his shoulder. "Excuse me sir," I say. "I think this belongs to you."

"Juliana!" Michael spins at the sound of my voice. "Oh my God, I found you!"

Technically it was the other way around, but I don't quibble. I place the fruitcake in his hands.

"Oh no you don't," he says, "You can't offload this baby until next Christmas."

I don't know what he sees on my face, but he doesn't get it right. No one could. He says, "You're not coming back are you?"

My forge-ahead future, so exciting a moment ago, smothers me with gray loneliness now that I see him. "Well, I don't know."

"It's X-It, isn't it? Is he going to be okay?"

I look straight into Michael's eyes. "I wish him the best," I say with honesty. "But I don't know, and I will never know. I won't be seeing him again."

Michael's voice takes on that fake-fatherly tone that used to irk me. Now I think it's funny. He takes off his glasses, wipes them with his jacket and says, "If you come back there's going to have be some changes."

"Hmm," I intone and allow him to ramble on about changes I was making anyway. His poor face. I want to make all that doubt go away.

"I don't think I can do this unless I can get you to promise a few things," he says. "You'll need to stay clean."

"Yup."

"You need to go to art school. Get a part-time job. Help with the bills."

"Yup. Yup. Yup."

"Stop it," he says, but he's grinning. "Come on, J.J., I need to know if you want to be the diamond I know you are?"

I take his glasses and put them back on his face. He's so corny. I can't help but give him my biggest Juliana Josephine Buckingham smile. "Just wait 'til I prove you right."

He beams back. "You know, we have a few days before you need to be back for school. I thought maybe you could show me your New York?"

I run my hand against his lightweight jacket. "We'll have to get the Californian a decent coat."

"Absolutely. And gloves." He nods like an eager kid. "And I want to see a musical, the museums, and the Statue of Liberty."

"I've never done any of those things," I say, "That's not my New York."

His fingertips wipe wetness from my cheekbone. "That can be our New York."

ABOUT THE AUTHOR

Jane George lives in the beautiful San Francisco Bay Area with her family and beloved kitty cats. She is a graduate of the California College of the Arts and holds a BFA in Illustration. She writes fiction and also young adult fantasy.

Read and see more at www.Jane-George.com

Printed in Great Britain
by Amazon